Oklahoma and Else

Oklahoma and Else

Stories

by

Paul H. Williams

Angelina River Press, LLC
Fort Worth, Texas

ISBN 978-0-9883844-6-0
Library of Congress Control Number:
2015932409

Angelina River Press, LLC
Fort Worth, Texas

Acknowledgments

I would like to thank the many friends and colleagues who have read and commented on the stories in this volume, as well as those who have given me support and encouragement. Among them are the late Bill Harrison, friend and mentor; Ellen Gilchrist, unfailing booster; Jim Morris, best of cheerleaders; Molly Giles, purveyor of tough love; Norm Snyder, sly and artful reader; Tom Wilkerson, good heartener; and David Kuhne, friend, editor, and reckless canoeist.

Paul H. Williams

For Allison

Contents

Jake Skin

Because of men, Jake Skin brought revenge into the world.

One day Jake Skin went fishing, and he fished and fished all up and down the big Blue River, and all he caught was a madtom, one eel, and two pumpkinseed perch. So he traveled far upstream until he came to a big fish weir made of willow sticks, and in it were what looked like all the bass and catfish in the river. A little farther along, Jake Skin came to a place in the river where the trotlines were so thick that only a madtom or an eel or a pumpkinseed perch could get through without getting caught. There were a hundred trotlines, bank to bank, every one with a hundred stages, every stage with a hundred hooks.

Jake Skin pulled up the lines and saw all the catfish, goggleye, and brown bass on them, and he thought: These men are too greedy. But since he could not take all the fish home for himself, he took enough for supper and let the others go.

Every day for three days, Jake Skin came back to let fish from the weir and off the hooks, but on the fourth day, someone saw him. The men had left one of theirs behind this time to watch the lines, and when they found out it was Jake Skin, they wanted to put an end to him and to his trickeries.

As Jake Skin walked along the trail to the river the next day, a rope snare snatched him by the feet, and Jake Skin was hanging upside down, surrounded by a bunch of men with angry, inverted faces. So Jake Skin laughed to see their scowls turned upside down. And then they all laughed at him, and he thought they were frowning.

Hanging like that, off of the ground, Jake Skin could not change his shape. He could only hang there and laugh, while the men whipped him with willow sticks and rot-ripened fish.

"There," they said, "take that, Jake Skin. We'll teach you to steal our fish, Jake Skin. You like a joke, Jake Skin. We will show you a good joke."

With that, the men dropped Jake Skin in a cow-hide sack and sewed him up inside. Being careful not to let it touch the ground, they carried Jake Skin to the river in the cow-hide sack and threw him in the water.

"You should get a good laugh out of that, Jake Skin," said the men. "What kind of fish will you be to swim out of that, Jake Skin?" And then they went away.

Jake Skin had never heard of a joke like this before, but he did not have to be any kind of fish to swim out of that sack. He took the knife out of his boot, cut through that cow-hide sack, and swam himself free. Then, since he was already wet, he paddled among the trotlines and cut them everyone and made big knots of them and made those knots into stone, for even though he enjoyed the fish, Jake Skin found that he liked this sort of joke just fine. So that is why we have Trotline Shoals in the Blue River today, why you can see the black shapes of fishhooks frozen in the white rocks of the rapids there.

Jake Skin went to his cabin and changed his clothes and sharpened his knife, then he went looking for the men who had snared him and beat him and laughed when they threw him in the river, for Jake Skin loved a good joke.

The men were having a big party that night on the stomp ground, eating fried fish, drinking chalk beer, and smoking tobacco. Jake Skin could hear them laughing and talking about him from a quarter-mile away. He sneaked all around the edge of the stomp, saw the men around the fires, dipping gourds in the crocks of beer, and he found where they had corralled their mules in a hollow on the other side of the ridge. Jake Skin cut himself a passel of greenbriars and sat down in the woods at the top of the ridge to wait.

After a while, all the men got drunk, some of them fought, then they all went to sleep, even the ones who were supposed to be watching the mules.

At first light, the men, who all had bad heads and sick stomachs, woke up to Jake Skin calling out to them from the top of the ridge.

"Hey, you men," he said. "Hey, you greedy men. You like a joke today? Your mules, they like a joke, too. Come on and see your mules laugh at my joke. Come see them smile like you."

And all the men jumped up, holding their heads, and ran to see what Jake Skin had done.

When they got to the corral, Jake Skin was already on the other side, throwing armloads of greenbriars in to the mules. He made the briars look like sweet clover to the mules, whose long, dangling ears he had shaved to sharp points. When the mules took up the clover, it was mean with thorns, and they made faces that looked like smiles, where Jake Skin had cut their mouths back nearly to their eyes.

"Oh, no, our beautiful mules have been maimed," said the men. "Look at their cropped ears. Look how they grin and chew greenbriars."

"Everybody likes a good joke," said Jake Skin. And he changed into a coyote and was gone.

And that is why to this day a mule will eat greenbriars and try to smile as it gnaws them, holding back its pointy ears in fear of Jake Skin's knife.

The Childs Daughter

Guess County, Oklahoma
December 1918
Ben Childs

Like that, like the dispatches that the Gist *Argus* used to reprint from France, with just the name of someplace you'd never heard before, then the date, and a list of the dead. After that, it's hard to know just where to start, though I suppose it has to start with Cora and those sorrows that the flu brought to her. To that I'd only add my own prayer for forgiveness.

Right now, with that child that I will someday, I'm sure, come to call my own, nestled between her breasts that have learned in but these three days to yield their clear witches' milk, I still know the sadness I felt at sight of her slim figure that morning before this just-passed storm, when I was debating whether or not to go to Ben Childs' place to bid his walnut. It came over me in a wink, but looking back, I can see it had been gathering all during those months of spring and summer and early fall when the flu marched through here. When it hit me that morning, it came down heavy as the sky, with its dark clouds slumping like patches of slag, ceiling-in the world. The light was just shifting to gray as I wrapped my hands around a second cup of coffee and stared out the kitchen window at that sky. Cora was leaned over the wet-sink, scraping our breakfast dishes, and as I glanced at her, it hit me, and I looked back out the window.

Her waist and hips were like a girl's, and Cora passing thirty-nine. It's gone ten years since anybody's kidded us about when were we going to start a family, but that had been a joke for so long that its bad ghost stayed on in folk's avoiding it. Especially when Cora's brothers and their wives and children would come over from Wagner, there always seemed to be a place in the conversation where that old joshing ought to fit, and everybody'd feel awkward and go quiet. But that morning I realized that Cora's glances at me in those silences were not to apologize for the awkwardness of her family but to thin out her own sorrow in mine. I all at once saw that, although we had never talked about it, what held us together was that guilt-sorrow we shared instead of a family.

That was one part of the sadness; the other was in knowing how alone we were, Cora and I, and how since the flu we'd even come to be without each other.

There was plenty of hard feeling toward me here after the mill shut down: the company left me as its purchasing agent, while most everybody else was out of work. After that, aside from Cora's family, we quit having what you could really call friends. It drew us closer for a while, made me long more than once every day to slide my arm around that small waist. But the flu soon put an end to that, too.

It was bad here when it finally came. They say it was worst on young men, like all those who died in the army camps, but in Guess County it was not so choosy. Cora nursed from house to house, after Doc Wickett died of it, but she couldn't do better than he did, and many did not survive, especially among the children. Then one morning she came in after a night too many of watching the fever burn out the light in children's eyes, and it was gone from hers, too. I'd sometimes find her after that crying at the sink, but when I'd reach to touch her, she'd say, "No. It's all right, Hank. I'm sorry. I just don't feel like a woman anymore."

So that morning, one part of me was hoping that the weather would turn for the worse, so I could, in good conscience, put off going to see Ben Childs, while another part prayed for the sky to clear, so I wouldn't have to face a day of excuses to keep myself outdoors.

Cora wrapped her tea towel around the handle of the coffee pot on the back of the stove, poured herself a cup, and came to sit with me at the table. She dripped coffee on the oilcloth as she sipped and didn't bother to wipe it up. Finally, she cut her eyes at me and asked, for the fourth or fifth time since the day before, "Have you decided?"

And for the fourth or fifth time, I told her, "I'm going to ask him to take market price for his timber."

She put down her cup and looked me full in the face. She said, "You could do it, Hank, if you would. You're the best at a bargain there is. You could make it sound like we were doing it special for him, or that he was obliging us—anything you want."

"Cora," I said, "if there was any one-other person buying, if the Devil himself was in the market, Ben Childs wouldn't sell me split-bark."

Cora picked up her cup and walked to the stove and back. "Can't you see it's not right, Hank?"

She turned away from him. Right?" I said. "*I've* got no right, Cora. Think about what you're saying."

"I think it's criminal not to."

"Is that what I ought to tell e and said, "Will it snow, do you think?"

I said it may, then scalded my mouth getting the coffee down, while Cora rattled her dishpans at me from the sink. I took my hat and long mackinaw off the back of the door and stepped outside into a mean wind that cut across the porch from the northeast, flattening the clumps of dead broom sage between our house—what had been the company office—and the stable that was once the engine shop, where Ben Childs' jackass locomotive had slept.

I'd given Sonny Bob, my gelding, a bucket of grain the night before, and he was restive in his stall, lifting his feet in place and tossing his head as I saddled him and looped the bridle over his ears. But he took the bit and didn't try to swell up on me when I drew the cinch tight. I led him out and tethered him to a porch post, then went in for my slicker and the .250-3000 Savage that I carry in the saddle boot.

Cora followed me back out on the porch, carrying a meal sack full of cold biscuits and sausage for my dinner and a syrup tin filled with water. I said, "Thank you, sweetheart," and kissed her on the lips. They were stung with cold, rough, and tight. "I ought to be back before supper."

I mounted Sonny Bob and reined him so hard that he reared as we wheeled, nearly taking my hat off on the eave of the porch. Cora stood silently, wrapped in her shoulder robe, as the wind struck tears from her eyes. The sky was seamless now.

"Better go inside," I said. "You'll catch cold in your eyes."

She pulled the shawl tighter and turned and went back in the house.

I rode north, following the trace of the old railbed that began behind the stable and scribbled its way through the washed-out, clear-cut ridges, toward a spur that would take me to Ben Childs' place, deep in the hills. *From whence cometh my help*, I remember thinking. Not that I really know scripture, just something that came to my mind. I rode hunched over the saddle horn, my hat bent low against the wind.

The tracks had been taken up three years before, and the rotting ties steadily since ground into the raised roadbed by mules and wagon rims and rain, leaving a sinking, shifting corduroy barely sound enough for a log-skid, when the run-off from the peeled ridges wasn't too great. The company built the railroad in the '90s, to haul in the white oak and hickory and walnut that we used to mill in what I now use as the timber depot, extending the line year by year until the ridges stopped them and the logs worth hauling fell farther and farther from the tracks. Ben Childs—who always called himself a "railroad man"—ran the wheezing wood-fired locomotive, with its open boiler and a wire cage for a cab. He nursed it, repaired it after two

8

derailments, even drew an extra dime a day for stoking it himself. But once the easy timber was gone, so was the short line and the mill. They pulled up the track and sold it for scrap. Those that could moved on when the company did, but most went back to hardscrabble farming, while some few retreated with the timber and the game deeper into the Cookson Plateau. They kept me on to see to the sale of the company buildings, and after that to buy up what little timber came out of the far hollows. And no one resented me more for that than Ben Childs, who simply squatted where he was left, moving his family into a line shack at the end of that track he once ruled from timber-docks to shop.

Losing that locomotive changed Ben, surled him, I would say. When the war came along, he went so far as to wonder out loud, to various ones within my hearing, why I, since I didn't have any kids, wasn't volunteering. There were plenty of men my age in the A.E.F., he said. But it didn't have a lot of bite, coming from Ben. By the very sight of him, Ben Childs was a beaten man. He began to drink some when he'd come to town, dragging his deep chest down into a paunch, and he was always in need of a shave. He took to silent spells of staring at his hands and arms, hatched black by the soot and sparks he had worked his extra dime a day for. That was the way he looked the first time he skidded logs down to the depot behind his span of fractious mules, following me around all during my measuring and reckoning, only looking up from those hands he kept turning in front of him long enough to cast a hard eye on my notebook.

But to my surprise, he didn't haggle, and took the first offer that I made.

"Well," I said, "that's easy done with, Ben. Care for a glass of lemonade?" I had a covered pitcher full that Cora had brought down from the house.

"The company still paying you for your time?" Ben asked me, examining his hands, front and back.

"Yeah," I said. "I suppose they are, Ben."

9

"Well," he said, dropping his hands, "they ain't me." He left without counting his money.

Sonny Bob broke stride and stopped, ears stiff, and I came up from my wool-gathering in time to see the white flag of a deer's tail sailing into the scrub along the roadbed. I eased the Savage out of the boot and slid to the ground behind a brake of red sumac, cradling the rifle across my knees and casting my eyes where I'd seen the deer disappear. For all the miles I ride through these hills, I seldom see a deer anymore, they having all been killed for meat by the logging crews, along with the turkey, or else moved to the marginal timber, along with the rest of the unlucky. The sight of one excited me and lifted my spirits. I sat still, feeling my cheeks go numb in the wind, then two more crossed, a doe and a yearling fawn. After another five minutes came the forkhorn buck. He paused on the crest of the roadbed, outlined against the gray sky, tasting the wind, and I shot him low behind the shoulder. I saw the hair fly where I hit him. He stiffened, arched his back, and jumped for the brush. But when he came down, his forelegs buckled, and he sprawled on his side, hind hooves scrabbling the flints.

I levered another round into the chamber and waited until he quit kicking before I stood. Twenty minutes later, with no tree big enough to hang him from, I had the deer bled and gutted on the sloping berm, his cavity propped open with sticks to let it glaze, while I stood in the lee of Sonny Bob, rinsed my hands from the syrup tin, and lit my pipe.

I was feeling good, as though the lean buck had somehow settled my quarrel with the world. I imagined the skinning and butchering, the canning and sausage-making to come. Cora dearly loves venison, and this would give her plenty to do to take her mind off things.

Plenty for Cora to do.

My mood passed. Cora, I knew, had plenty to do. What she wanted was a baby, and to her mind, Ben Childs had one extra. It seemed simple to her; two plus two equals. What she couldn't see was how things stood between Ben and me, that I had no handle on him. She was just overcome with a kind of nervous grief, following all those deaths, I told myself. And how many *extra* can there be, after all those tiny coffins? But in her practical, woman's way, she was right. There was no good sense in the thought of Ben Childs trying to raise a baby alone in that old line shack.

I recalled clearly that day this past May when Ben Childs brought his own wife, Modean, down to the town to be buried. She was one of the first to die, and there were those who would believe that it was she who brought the influenza to us. It was just Ben Childs' foul luck to have that sort of unkindness piled on him, after what must have been a grim trip for him and his kids down to the communities along the Blue.

There was a long spell of rain at the end of an otherwise dry spring this year, and during it, only a good rider on a sound mule could have negotiated the gullies and sucking mud of the roadbed. So, when Modean fell ill, Ben had no choice but to tend her himself, while his oldest child, a girl about twelve, looked to the other four kids. They watched their mother wither for a week, shriveling beneath the fever, then, as so many do, void herself onto the mattress before she died.

Ben had no lumber for a coffin, but I'm sure it was with a reverence that he folded Modean into a flour barrel, lidded it tight, hammered down the bands, and caulked the seams with tar. Still, when they came down at last into the depot yard in their muddy wagon drawn by Ben's two anvil-headed mules, the smell was overpowering and unmistakable. Ormand or Orlund—one or the other of the young twins sitting with Ben on the wagon seat—said to me when I came out into the depot yard, "Our mama's goin' to heaven. She needs a bath, 'cause she's goin' to heaven."

I leaned against Sonny Bob's neck, thinking, "And to the little fellow, that was a real place."

The Childs stayed a week or so with his nephew's wife, out near New Echota, so they were there when word came of the nephew's death from the flu at the Army camp where he was making ready for France. Then, his wife died of it too, leaving Ben Childs with their three-month old baby to take with him back to the shack. Ben could have stayed in the valley and made a living-wage as a mechanic, if he hadn't been so damned stiff-necked about being a railroad man.

With our own epidemic at hand, I never called Ben Childs to mind, though I now realize how terrible it must have been for him. Those odd acres of clear-cut that he was trying to farm would yield only in patches, and seemed to begrudge every potato, melon, and ear of corn that the bugs or coons didn't get. And every time he'd skid another log in for ready cash, there was a dead child with it, until they numbered five, the last one only two weeks ago. That was when he told me, "Sams, if you want that 'ere fine walnut, you're gonna have to come out to bid it. That off-mule a mine's done cracked a hoof."

So it was, that, with quotas for the company to meet, I was riding into the wind again, with the deer draped over Sonny Bob's withers, feeling for Ben Childs something almost like sympathy. But that feeling wouldn't last. By the time I got to Boneyard spring and stopped for Sonny Bob to water, the wind had shifted to due north, bringing the smell of snow, and I still had most of an hour before I'd reach the end of the line. I ate some sausage and a biscuit and rode on, sour with the world, the goddamn war, the shutdown, the influenza, and Ben Childs' fine goddamn walnut.

It's my own mean vanity had done it, of course. When Ben brought his last log and child down, he also skidded in a butt-slice of black walnut nearly seven-feet across, offering it as a sample of what he had on the ground back at his place. I told Ben that I'd come out to take a look at it, trying to act casual about the prospect. But the dirty truth is, I had got caught up in a fancy, the notion of seeing myself photographed next to that huge butt-slice, my timber brand in hand, leaning against the giant sawlog on its skid. Even as I wished it, I knew it was fond-foolish and vain, but I couldn't keep that picture from my mind. I never mentioned it to Cora, for each time I thought I might, that urge got snuffed out by the sadness that'd settled around her, one deeply at odds with my small desire.

At the end of the line, the roadbed disappears into a gullied delta of scrub and red mud in a clearing where a roundabout used to be, and at the edge of it, sitting cocked on a foundation of stumps, is the line shack that Ben Childs called home. Patches of sumac and persimmon had taken hold around the cabin. In the clearing where Ben had grubbed out stumps, dark water stood in ragged craters, like the shell-holes across No-Man's Land that we all saw in the *Illustrated Weekly*. The rust streaks in the valleys of the shack's corrugated roof dripped down the unpainted sides, and there was greased paper in place of glass in most of the window sash. The wire gate to the mule corral was down.

I was letting Sonny Bob pick his way among the stump holes, circling wide toward the shack, when I saw the walnut that I'd ridden out in a coming storm to bid. It was a damned crotch-log. The butt-section I had seen and pinned my vanity on was from a trunk not four feet long. Beside it lay the two forks of the crotch, usable timber, but nothing that would have brought me out on even a good day. I knew it served me right, though that did not much lessen my resentment, and I cursed Ben Childs roundly in my mind.

As I came up to the shack I called out, "Hello, the house. Anybody home?" There was movement behind one piebald window. The warped door jerked once and then came open, scraping on the sill. Ben Childs looked out at me, at the deer, and said, "You shoot somebody's pet, Sams?"

"Down by Boneyard," I said. "Had to. Self-defense."

13

Ben's laugh was hollow, mocking me. He turned his eyes toward the dark shapes of the walnut on the ground and said, "I guess now you really don't know what you're doin' here, do you? Do you, Henry Sams? Well, get down and come on in, then, long as you are."

There was a lean-to shed on the lee side of the shack, where I hung the deer by all-fours from a purlin and tethered Sonny Bob away from it, then went back to the front and mounted the stump that served as a porch and knocked.

Ben called from inside, "Not locked."

I shouldered open the door and stepped inside It took me a beat or two to realize that the light was wrong. Ben must have had his every lamp and lantern lit, even the ceiling fixture, with its brass reservoir and tinted-glass shade, like he owned shares in kerosene. And knowing Ben as I did, I wouldn't have expected to see headboards and bedding neatly stacked in a corner, the floor swept, and the one standing bed spread with a Dutch-girl quilt. Beside it was a slatted cradle with a blanketed lump inside.

"Picked a hell of a day, didn't you?" Ben said. "Take off your coat and have a seat."

He had been cleaning his shotgun on the table. He picked up the stock, barrel, and forearm and put them, along with the rags and oil, on a kitchen commode next to a dented pitcher-set.

"No coffee," Ben said. "Got sassafras, if you want something hot. Whiskey if you don't."

"I'd appreciate a cup of 'fras," I said.

The whole place was bright as brass and smelled fresh of oil-soap. There was a pot and a kettle on the stove, and the room was hot as hell in the summertime. I unbuttoned my mack, hung it over a ladderback chair, and sat down. Ben took the kettle off the iron flat-top, filled two tin cups with water and orange shavings of sassafras that he kept in a sugar bowl, then put one of the cups in front of me and sat down himself across the table in the only other chair. I tried to scoot closer, but my chair was fast to the floor.

"She's nailed," Ben said. He turned one hand and studied it, then turned and looked at me. Ben was smooth shaven. I could smell the white whiskey on him.

"Know yet why you're here, Henry Sams?"

"Somebody's idea of a joke, maybe."

Ben Childs spread his hands on the table and looked down at them. "How 'bout that walnut?"

"Not worth the ride out here, Ben. And you goddamn well know it."

"Well, I got some meat stew, then, if you're hungry. Old mule eats pretty good, if'n you cook him long enough. Sure you don't want a drink?"

It wasn't just that he was drinking before noon or that he and the place were both glaring clean, nor that he was being the way I had come to expect of him. I just felt that Ben was circling on something that had to do with me being there, and nothing to do with timber. And I didn't like it.

I heard a movement in the crib and said, "How's that baby, Ben? Y'all doing all right?"

"Sassafras and sugar-tit for her, meat stew and whiskey for me. Sure, we're doin' fine."

"Thought maybe you could use a haunch of that venison I shot."

Ben held one hand down with the other, looked at me, and sat back in his chair with that same gaze as when he stared at his hands. "A man," he said, "ain't got no soul—you know that, Sams?— no, nor woman neither. Not no soul of your own, leastways. Listen now: all that-there belongs to God, and what we got is just a little piece on loan, like, seeing how we turn a profit on it or not. Time comes, it all goes back to Him, same as the bank or commodities store always gets its own, one way or t'other. Ain't nothing of it ours, no more'ns in that deer meat acrost your saddle. Whose deer was that, anyways, afore you shot him? What the hell do you know?"

"Cora said to say that she'd be much obliged to look after the baby for you, just until spring, maybe. 'Til you can get back on your feet."

He stared at his hands and said, "How 'bout that walnut?" Then he laughed.

"Ben," I said, "I'm here, and I'll buy your goddamn stove wood, and I'll even get the Fulbright boys to skid it out when they come up this way next. But this is the last business you and me'll ever do together. You understand?"

"Oh, you're right on that, Henry Sams," he said. "I'm gettin' out of it. You're right on that. Now, 'bout that walnut."

I put on my coat and went outside to grade and measure the wood. The wind was steady from the north now, shooting needles of sleet. It wasn't a quarter hour to calculate the usable yield from the walnut. I wrote Ben a chit, using Sonny Bob's saddle for a desk, then retightened the cinch, took the deer from the purlin, and rode around to the front, where Ben Childs was waiting in the open door.

He took the chit, tucked it in the bib of his overalls, and handed me a pint fruit-jar with an inch of clear liquor in it. "Can't leave 'til we drink to that walnut," he said.

I took a sip and squinted at the burn, begrudging myself for wanting it. When I tried to hand him back the jar, Ben Childs said, "No. You drink it down."

I put the jar back to my lips, and he went on, "I never did like you, Henry Sams. Not one damn bit. You never was no railroad man, but I got too much to get done around here, gettin' ready for spring and all. Don't you say a goddamn word. This here's what I had you out for."

He took the jar from me and reached behind the door.

I turned in the saddle and slid my hand to the rifle stock behind my right thigh.

Ben came up with the bundle of blanket that I'd seen in the crib.

"How 'bout this, Henry Sams?" he said. "What would the world think of something so pretty as this?"

"Ben," I said. "Just wait a minute."

"Well," he said, "I don't give a damn what you think."

He held out the baby to me.

"Just 'til spring," he said. "Take her, damn you, or they won't be no goddam walnut neither."

I took the bundle from Ben's hands. He looked at them, empty there in space, while I buttoned the baby inside my belted mackinaw.

"Snow's coming," he said. "Just one thing more."

He pushed the door part-way closed as he stepped behind it. "Sams," he said from inside, "pull my door shut, will ye?"

I leaned out in one stirrup, caught the loop of leather in my hand, and straightened, drawing the door over the sill.

The roar of the shotgun sent Sonny Bob leaping to the side, where he landed stiff-legged and started to buck.

I bunched the reins and held the bundled baby tight beneath my coat with one arm, while my other hand clawed for my rifle. My horse came around, and I stopped.

I turned Sonny Bob and swung to the muddy earth and went inside. Ben Childs was dead at the table. The shotgun, with a cord tied from its trigger to the door, was lashed to the back of the chair I'd sat in, pointing at Ben's shattered chest. An unfired shotgun shell lay on the floor beneath his blackhatched hand. Blood dripped from the chair beside it.

Oh, Ben," I said out loud. "Ben, you son of a bitch, what have you done to yourself?" But I think I meant, "to me?"

I picked up the unspent shell, cut the gun free, laid it on the table, and put the shell and the cords in my pocket.

17

What had this sad hull of a man done to me? What had he been thinking? Was Ben Childs trying to make it look that I'd murdered him? For who'd believe what had really happened? And if not, why me? Was this his way of finally getting at me? By making him my guilt? It was damnedable to think so of a dead man, but I could not help it. What would anyone think? And why would they not? What else could I do? What less than save myself? I moved the gun into his hand.

I damned Ben Childs again as I stepped out onto the stump. I mounted Sonny Bob where he stood at rein, leaned out for the leather strap, and drew it to. The door screeched over the sill and fell shut.

I rode until we were back on the railbed before I stopped, with the wind at my back, to see what I had. The baby was thin and looked fretful in sleep. As I tucked the scrap of blanket back around her, I saw lap-embroidered in one corner the names *Benjamin* and *Modean*. The wind snapped my collar like a shot.

By the time I reached home, the snow was beginning to slacken and the mercury to drop. But inside the kitchen, Cora was aglow. I tremble to think how she held me and cried, how purely happy she was turning a rubber glove into a nipple, fashioning a crib from an empty flour-drawer in the kitchen safe, how she insisted on getting out the feather bed and making us a pallet on the kitchen floor, so we could sleep in the same room as our daughter on her first night at home.

We lay there in the dark, each of us, I know, with thoughts we were not sharing. The baby stirred, and Cora said to me, "What kind of man, Henry Sams, would give away something as wonderful as this? You know he won't be coming for her in the spring. Oh, Hank, how can you do dealings with men of such black stamp? How could Ben Childs ever love something like this?"

I haven't yet told Cora what the Fulbright boys found up there this morning: Ben Childs dead, one spent shell in his gun marked with his name. Suicide, they say. On the shell that I got from Ben's floor was written the name *Julianna*, that of the child he had given me. Of course, Cora will have to know about Ben's death, but it's probably best she doesn't know it all. She'd never believe that Ben Childs ate his last mule out of pity, just to see it didn't starve to death.

Seeds in the Cellar

The rosy-brown water of Boneyard Creek curled like a question mark in the eddy where it flowed into the Little Blue. It arced with the counter current, circled the pool, then tailed downstream into invisibility. Tandy Gourd stood in the clear, stonedimpled current below the pool, squinting across its surface. The day was growing hot, and he wore no shirt. Half-floating beside him was the gray wasp nest he had knocked from the eave of the well house and pinned to a belt loop on his jeans. Holding his pole beneath his arm, he peeled the seal off one of the paper cells and thumbed out a yellow pupa. It flexed and straightened between his fingers. He examined its opaque, bulbous eyes, the creases that scored its yellow abdomen, and threaded it on his hook. He used no weight on his line, only the long-shanked hook and the bait and three feet of leader, just the way Papa Gourd had taught him. He surveyed the surface of the riffling pool, took his rivercane pole in both hands, and flipped the line in a lazy arc, dropping the bait gently to dot the question mark.

The pupa bobbed uncertainly for a moment, then the weight of the line and the slow curl of the mingling streams dragged it under. The line unfolded its floating loops, straightened, sagged suddenly, and then went taut. Tandy raised the tip of his pole and held it high as he backed into the shallows. In less than a minute, he was prying the hook from the jaw of a wriggling brown bass and slipping it into a dented lard can to join the half-dozen others he had caught.

He cleaned his fish in the shallows with a pocket knife, watching the soft gray and pink folds of their entrails coil in the clear water, their feathered gills in bloom. Fish scales like chips of rainbow washed away downstream.

Tandy had always loved his summers in Guess County but now wished more than ever before that he had Papa Gourd here to talk with about what he saw. When he was young, he would always talk about what he saw, never imagining he was any different, that others did not see things as he did, that they did not feel the deep, uncertain meaning in seeing a bird with only one leg or in the shape of water over rocks or in the flowering of fish gills. Papa Gourd, his grandfather, had seemed to understand, allowing Tandy to feel in conspiracy with the world in a way that he no longer did. With Papa, Tandy could share a sense of wonder when the old man said, "Sure is lots of different kind of birds, ain't they?" They had buried Papa Gourd last winter, just before Washington's Birthday, and Tandy had never wept for him.

He lay his fish in a row on a rock and looked at them: seven slim bass of all the same size, more than a mess for him and Granny May.

When Tandy reached the road at the top of the ridge above the creek, Granny May was on the front porch running laundry through the wringer of the washing machine, the same one Tandy had seen her load with poke greens in the spring and use to rinse and spin the dirt from them. Today, she was wringing sheets into a basket, easing them through the clamped rollers with her long hands. Tandy had never thought it odd that she was bigger than Papa Gourd—tall and big-chested and taciturn—because she had such small wrists and tapered, finely-turned hands that looked ignorant of iron skillets or lye soap or the hickory-limb handle of her garden hoe.

"T-Boy," she said to him, "better soak some coal-oil on him wast nest. Them things'll hatch out, otherwise. You got enough for us and Miz Birdsong too? She's comin' over at lunch."

"I got seven," he said, as he put down the lard can and unpinned the wasp nest from his waist. He dropped the nest on the porch beside the can and laid the fish out side-by-side.

"That's nice, T-Boy. Those some nice *atsadi*." said Granny May. She lowered a damp flap of sheet into the basket. "All pan-size. That'll be plenty. Him good today, that goin' to water?"

Tandy always felt uneasy when Granny May spoke that way of old customs and used Cherokee names for things, a way he never had with Papa Gourd.

"All I did was go fishing, Granny May," he said, raking the fish back into the can.

"You got a place to go to water in Tulsa?"

"Yeah," Tandy said. "We call it a bath tub, Granny May."

She fed another sheet into the electric wringer and looked at him, her eyes betraying nothing. "Go rub some vinegar on," she said. "Get that fish off you hands."

The old part of the house was a hewn-log dogtrot chinked with white mortar. Papa Gourd had added two clapboard wings, one for a kitchen and bath, the other for two bedrooms, and on the back a screened porch made of cedar posts and warped oak planks worn to the contours of their grain by three generations of bare feet and mail-order brogans. The house had a pressure system, but Papa Gourd plumbed only the kitchen; Granny May had to carry water from there to fill the bathtub or flush the toilet. Papa bathed year-round in a galvanized tub on the back porch and always used the privy. Twice a day he drew his drinking water from the well by hand and kept it in a tin pail on the porch, covered with a tea towel.

Tandy stood on the porch, scrubbing his hands and arms with white vinegar, surrounded by his grandfather's relics, his fishing poles and his kindling hatchet and a three-legged milking stool. Nailed to one post was the mummified head of the giant catfish that Papa had caught, its stiff, ropey whiskers curled like a gambler's. Tandy still had the clipping from the *Argus*, a picture of Papa Gourd holding the catfish head-high, its tail just touching the ground. The caption beneath the photo read, "John Gourd of Melonvine—what a catch!" Papa's milking clothes—the hat and overalls—still hung from one post on a stob of limb. The old fedora was worn smooth on one side, mangled with cow hair, the overalls frayed almost to the knees.

Tandy lifted the scrap of calico covering the water pail and rinsed his arms with a gourd dipper, watching the water cup in the floorboards and run through the cracks between them onto the bare earth beneath. He emptied the rest of the pail on the floor and watched the water disappear.

Tandy took the pail and went to the well to refill it. Papa had built the tiny well house out of stone, and it was cool inside. Tandy let the chain rattle through the pulley as he lowered the bucket, listened as it gurgled and filled, then hoisted the wet chain back up. He rested the long, cylindrical bucket on the edge of the well casing and pulled the ring in the top to release the water. It fell in a cold rush into the pail that Tandy braced between his Keds, blossoming from the mouth of the bucket and over the lip of the pail onto his feet. Outside the well house, he heard the one-legged catbird call.

Growing up in the city, Tandy had played all the games that children play, but he always felt he was playing false when the game was Wild West, and he had to be an Indian. The narrow face that he saw in the mirror, with its downturned mouth and high cheek bones, was not the face he imagined for himself. Inside, he dreamed of Kit Carson, Davy Crockett, Wyatt Earp. He could not understand why he had to be an Indian. His father was a foreman at the refinery; his mother taught typing at the Triple-A Business School. They listened to Patsy Cline and Carl Perkins. It confused Tandy to play an Indian. He was not the same in that world as he was with Papa Gourd, where he didn't have to pretend.

Since he was five, Tandy had spent nine summers with his grandparents in the hills above the Little Blue. Usually there was a rotating cast of cousins for him to play with, but he was always the one who stayed the longest, who was there when the others had gone. He was the one Papa Gourd taught to milk and thread pipe and use wasp larvae for bait. Papa Gourd would say, "That's him cat, *achucha*, what the Cherokee calls *wesa*." Or, "That's him *aliga*, what we call that red-horse fish. *Golisdi*?"

Tandy did understand. He understood that the world lived in two places, that Guess County was a world different from Tulsa, and that the things of this place had different names in the world that lived here. And so did he, many names. To Papa, he was just boy, *achucha*. To himself, he was sometimes secretly Gourd Rattler, a shaman superhero who could change into a snake. To the cousins, he was Tandy or, to the teasing girls, Dandy. Only Granny May called him T-Boy. She began when he was no more than seven, sitting beside him in the porch swing as she stroked his head.

"Tulsa," she said. "T-Town. You the T-Town Boy. We'll call you T-Boy, to make it short."

"T-Boy," Granny May called from the screened porch. "T-Boy, come on for lunch and put you a shirt on. Miz Birdsong's here to see us."

Beulah Birdsong was his grandmother's oldest friend, a tiny woman with sharp movements and a measured, knowing smile that always made Tandy ill at ease. She and Granny May sometimes spoke in Cherokee, and the way she smiled made Tandy sure they were talking about him, especially when they would laugh so deep and satisfied, holding their fingers to their lips like girls. She called him *achucha*, too, just like Papa Gourd, except when she spoke to Granny May. Then she would say, "Look how your T-Boy's growin'." Or, "Your T-Boy bein' good?"

The adults that Tandy was drawn to, the kind he knew would one day be his friends, were those who knew what to say to right a situation. It was not that they said clever things or things that showed how much they knew. No, it was those who knew the words to calm a

25

fear, to gentle an awkward moment, to make a stranger feel at ease. To Tandy, Miz Birdsong was none of these.

Tandy put on dry jeans and a shirt and went into the kitchen, where Miz Birdsong sat at the table, talking to Granny May, who stood at the stove. The room smelled of hot grease and fry bread and boiled, bitter greens. A sugar bowl, a salt-and-pepper set, a pitcher of tea, a lump of churned butter, and jars of pickled vegetables crowded the middle of the table. There were places laid for four.

"'*Chucha*," said Miz Birdsong, holding out one leathery arm, "come let's have a look at you, see how much you grown in a week."

Tandy let her squeeze his arm and shoulder. He stood very straight and grinned uneasily. "Who else is coming?" he said, nodding toward the extra plate.

Miz Birdsong took her hand off him and looked at Granny May, who turned from the stove with a plate of fried fish in her hand and said, "That's for your Papa Gourd, T-Boy. For his birthday today. You get us some ice for the tea."

Tandy cracked the cubes from two ice trays and filled four glasses with warm, sweetened tea. He burned with shame. Was this Papa Gourd's birthday? And how had he not known?. Was he forgetting him already? He felt miserably alone and trapped in the low, hot room with Miz Birdsong and Granny May, gnawed by the memory that he had never grieved for Papa Gourd. He had felt sad, lonesome, uncertain, but he had not cried, not even at the funeral, when all the rest were bent with grief. He sometimes thought it was because he had not loved Papa Gourd enough, not as much as his uncles or cousins or aunts. He knew nothing about this dumb ritual of Granny May's, but it seemed meant to torment him with his failing, to punish him with the abashed presence of memory.

Granny May served them each two fish, placing the seventh on the extra plate.

"Mister John, he's eatin' light nowadays," Miz Birdsong said.

"That's right," said Granny May. She touched her lips with her fingertips. "Remember how much that little man could eat?"

"Deer meat," said Miz Birdsong brightly, pressing her own lips to contain a snicker.

Tandy wished his head would sink between his shoulders, go to rest in the darkness inside his chest.

"Sit down, T-Boy," said Granny May. "You got a fever, Sweetheart?"

"I'm fine, Granny May."

"Then you sit next your Papa Gourd and me."

Tandy sat across from Miz Birdsong, the empty seat to his right, forked a gob of turnip greens onto his plate, and poured pickled-pepper brine over them and the fish.

Granny May exchanged a glance with Miz Birdsong, put a plate of frybread on the table, and settled in her chair.

"Say our prayers now, T-Boy."

Tandy said grace rapidly, but had to hold a long breath before Granny May would say, "Amen."

"Amen," Miz Birdsong repeated. "You like you Papa John, *achucha*," she said to Tandy. "He didn't like no long prayers either—did he, Sister Gourd?"

"Mister John never got him real religion, not when I had deer meat on the table."

Miz Birdsong tittered. "Dear me, deer meat," she said through her fingers. "Dear God, let's eat."

"Beulah," said Granny May. "You stop that."

Miz Birdsong said something in Cherokee, and both of them laughed.

Tandy filleted a fish with his fork and laid the skeleton whole on the edge of his plate. Miz Birdsong slurped greens from a spoon. Granny May broke off a crisp tail and nibbled it from her fingers.

"Granny May," said Tandy, staring at his food, "why'd you set a place for Papa?"

"It's what we do, *'chucha*," said Miz Birdsong. "Him *adanta* still here until that first birthday after you die. This our last time to talk with him. You say what you want."

"T-Town Boy don't like them old-time things," said Granny May, licking grease from her fingers. "Him goes to water in that bathtub. Don't you, T-Boy?"

"Stop it, Granny May."

"You go ahead; talk to you Papa Gourd."

Miz Birdsong spoke to the empty air in Cherokee. Granny May nodded and repeated a word beneath her breath, as though correcting her friend.

"Don't scold at him," she said to Miz Birdsong. "Him will always know that last thing you say."

"Granny May," said Tandy, "I'm not hungry. Can I be excused?"

"That's why he never married you," Granny May said to Miz Birdsong. And to Tandy: "Don't you be rude too, T-Boy. This what you Papa John him wanted. Just this and him dipper gourds. It's not so much." She stared at Miz Birdsong.

"What dipper gourds?" he said.

"He knows I'm just for fun," said Miz Birdsong. She brushed Granny May's words away with the back of her hooked hand. "Those old seed gone bad by now, anyhow." She raked a spoon across her plate.

"You promised them seed, Beulah Birdsong. Him knows you did."

"Could've took better care of you own. You wouldn't leave 'em in those gourds, like I say."

Miz Birdsong scooped another spoon of greens into her mouth.

Tandy said, "Can I be excused?"

Granny May looked at him, at Miz Birdsong, then back at Tandy. "Where them seed, Beulah?" she said.

28

"I hung you a string on the porch," Miz Birdsong said. "So there." She turned her wicked grin on Tandy. "You remember now whose seed gonna grow you Papa John's dipper-gourd vines, *achucha*."

"Poo," said Granny May. "Them's his gourd seed, same as I raised him forty years."

"Rattle the same as you tongue," said Miz Birdsong.

Tandy scrooched down in his chair.

"T-Boy," said Granny May. "Go see what this old woman left on my porch, and bring it back in here."

Tandy scraped his chair away from the table and slouched out of the kitchen. He was embarrassed and not a little confused. He had never seen Granny May like this, arguing in front of Papa. *Papa?* He stopped and looked back to the kitchen. From this angle he could not see Miz Birdsong or Granny May, only his own empty chair and the one at the end of the table, where a shadow moved once and was gone.

The nape of Tandy's neck was tingling as he walked out the front door. A bundle of dry dipper gourds tied up with twine hung from one porch post. He gathered them in his arms and took them to the kitchen.

"Those the children of that first vine," Miz Birdsong said.

"Same as mine," said Granny May. She made room on the table and untied the gourds and shook each one of them by her ear. She chose two and handed them to Tandy.

"These the ones you have," she said. "These your seeds from Papa Gourd, T-Boy. Like that old woman say, they the children of the children of that first vine, pass down from seeds come all the way on that Trail of Tears, you know. You make him dippers from those and plant they seed."

"That's right, *'chucha*," Miz Birdsong said. "Ever year now you grow that vine that go back to Echota, back east to the peace town where they bad men give it all away. That way, you Papa John always be with you."

"Tell him, 'Thank you,'" said Granny May.

Miz Birdsong grunted and said, "Should tell him to thank me."

"Someday," said Granny May, "you get that bone hung in you throat, Beulah Birdsong. Eat you fish. T-Boy, you be excused long enough to take him gourds to the cellar. Then get you right back."

Tandy gathered the gourds and walked out to the side of the house where the storm cellar was dug into the face of the ridge, its low, Z-braced door set in an upright slab of concrete. He laid the gourds on the ground, setting his two apart, slipped the barrel-bolts loose, and pulled the door open by its handle of braided bailing wire. He knelt and searched the inside with his eyes—snakes sometimes found their way in here to cool—then picked up the gourds and ducked through the door, blinking into darkness. He stood shivering for a moment as the shelves and benches took their shapes. There was not much in the cellar at this time of year—a few jars of pickles and jam, a burlap bag sprouting iris roots, a box of wax candles, and matches in a snuff tin. Tandy lit one of the yellowed candles and dripped a puddle on a shelf to set it in.

He found a place for Granny May's gourds and picked up his two, one in each hand. He shook them by his ears, wondering what Granny May had heard in them. One sounded hard, the seed like field peas in a can; the other's note was deeper, muffled, as though the seed had fur. He shook them together, then one at a time, collecting a rhythm. He began to move his feet as he shook them. There was a swelling in his chest, something of anger and something of release. He bowed his head and danced: Gourd Rattler. He lifted his knees high and moved in a small circle, shaking the gourds and chanting, "YA-ya, YA-ya, YA-ya, YA-ya...."

When Tandy at last stopped, the sweat was cold on the back of his neck and tears ran in sheets on his cheeks. "Cochise," he cried hoarsely. "Stand Watie. Papa Gourd." He did not know where his anger pointed, whom it accused, what he could strike to end it. He felt he was a fraud, an impostor wherever the world lived. In his mind, he cried to Papa Gourd that he was sorry. Then it was done, and his arms felt like dead wood, his hands grown to the gourds. There was snot on his lip, but he could not raise his arm to wipe it.

Tandy began to tremble violently, his sobbing reduced to a dry hack. His knees folded, and he went to them on the cool earth of the cellar floor. Memories flashed like a thousand snapshots, making his grandfather whole in a kinescope of time, flickering but complete in every motion: washing the cow's udder, guiding a hand plow behind Old June, lining up a squirrel in the sights of a .22, splitting kindling for the fire. Tandy could smell dusty summer woods, dew on honeysuckle, wet cow, and fish being cleaned by the river. He wiped his lip on his wrist, put aside his gourds, and shuffled out into the light.

He went to the clothes line and wiped his face on one of the sheets that Granny May had hung out to dry. He smelled the sunshine and the bleach. He felt exhilarated, emptied of something. He had to will his feet not to fly, force them to walk to the porch, where a newly hatched wasp staggered in a strip of sunlight, fanning its wings in spasms. Another whipped side to side as it struggled damply from its cell. He liked that, and liked the idea that the rest of them would hatch before Miz Birdsong left. Wasp: *Kanatsisdetsi*: the longest word he knew.

Solace

The auctioneer's voice rattled through the loudspeaker a second time: "Seventeen. Lot seventeen, into the pit."

Joshua Lookingglass rose unsteadily to his feet beside the gate to pen seventeen, into the heat pulsing from the auction barn's corrugated sheet-iron sides. It was cooler down by the floor of the aisle, down by the mud and manure and hay, where he had dropped the battery cap. He leaned heavily on the gate post, a tall, big-bellied man the color of old pennies wearing only Salvation Army brogans and a pair of bib overalls. His thick, scarred hands felt indistinct, senseless as sponge, but he had managed fresh batteries into his cattle prod.

"Lot seventeen,"

The bald yard-boss squinted up from his clipboard and started down the long aisle of pens toward seventeen. Joshua grimaced at a sour bay-rum belch and fumbled open the hasp of the heifers' pen. Holding the gate to block the aisle and chute the cattle to the auction pit, he leaned over the top and prodded one of them in the flank. Nothing. Joshua stabbed at the button on his prod. He could feel the yard-boss coming. He clubbed the nearest heifer across the back with the heavy capacitor-end of his prod. She snorted, jumped awkwardly to one side and looked at him. Joshua licked his lips and stared blankly at the prod. The battery cap, he saw, was cross-threaded.

"Move 'em out, Chief," the yard-boss called, not as near as Joshua had thought.

Clenching the sweaty prod between his knees, he wrenched the cap loose, aligned the threads, cinched it tight, and hit his leg with the prongs and the button with his thumb almost at once. The shock arced through his groin and hit his queasy belly like a kick.

"Seventeen, into the pit. A dozen Brahma-Shorthorn cross heifers. Good-looking stock, boys."

Doubled over against the gate, Joshua thrust blindly between the slats of the fence. A dappled, lop-eared heifer bolted from the hot prongs, hit the gate, and sent Joshua sprawling at the yard-boss's feet.

The yard-boss took off his straw Stetson and wiped his bald skull with a blue bandana. "Chief," he said, "you better let me show you how to use that thing."

"'M all right," Joshua said, bracing the gate with one brogan. He pushed up on his elbow and held out the cattle prod. "I got him fixed now."

"I thought you told me you worked cows before, Chief."

"I can work cows. Good at cows. Always worked cows."

A lanky boy with a cratered face walked over from eighteen, pushed his hat back with his cattle prod, and said, "Yeah, you worked that hot-shot real slick, Chief."

"I ain't no chief, son," Joshua said as he climbed up the gate to his feet.

"You ain't worked no cows before neither, Chief," the yard-boss said. He wiped his head again. "What kinda fool you take me for?"

Joshua mumbled to the fence, "How many is they?"

The yard-boss's wattled neck stiffened and his bald head glowed. "Chief," he said, settling his Stetson, "I'm gonna scalp you from asshole to appetite if you said what I think."

Joshua faced him and stepped away from the gate, rolling the cattle prod lightly between his thumb and fingers. "Shit," he said.

The yard-boss took a short step and snatched the prod from his hand.

Joshua, startled at the old man's quickness, flinched away into the hot-shot prongs the boy from eighteen drew across his bare back.

He bit his tongue, cracked his back as he whipped around and slid into a spraddle-legged fighter's stance. Joshua glared at the white men, the yard-boss' mottled forehead fragile as a blown egg.

The yard-boss edged closer to the lanky boy. "Lookingglass," he said, "you kin go get your check. Six hours' worth, you hear.

Joshua yawed in his thick shoes. "You sendin' me home?" he said.

"I think he means now," said the boy from eighteen.

Joshua drew his pay and walked out the back of the auction barn to where a twisted trailer frame sat rusting on four concrete blocks. He needed a drink to balance his having drawn a short check. Papa John, his stepdaddy, had paid for the calf Joshua killed last year, and another full week at the auction barn could have finally squared the debt. Now there would be the guilt, Papa's questions without answers. And because of them, and because he had been ripe to ambush the yard-boss and didn't, Joshua felt he needed—no, deserved—whatever release a drink, made necessary by a hundred hundred other drinks, might give. It was just that: only the necessary drink: not like really drinking at all.

Joshua leaned on the rust-scaled trailer frame, wiped sweat from his lips, and slipped a flat whiskey bottle from one of the hollow blocks. He shook the inch of liquid in the bottom of the bottle—cut one part to five with bay rum cologne—and a sweet-hot belch broke in his gullet. He wanted his hands to stop shaking, but he could not, could not, put that bottle to his lips. If he ought to have a drink, he had money now. Even change from the bay rum. He marveled at his trembling hand until the sun began to beat on the back of his head. The clock on the Gist courthouse tower struck, and in that moment Joshua heard Papa John asking where the money was. He looked up the shimmering black band of highway to the first ridge of the scrubby hills, to a break in the trees where the town began. Three leaden peals:

four o'clock or maybe four-thirty. The clock was always slow. Punk's had been open for at least an hour.

Beneath the heat, Joshua thought of the asphalt's dusty shoulder on the steep grade into town. He looked at the bottle in his hand. Circling town at the foot of the hills, fording Little Sandy Creek where it turned west from south, and cutting across two pastures and a patch of woods, he could get to the head of the hollow that led to the highway that went to Dallas if you were lucky and Arkansas if you were not—the highway where Punk's was—without crossing a single paved road.

Joshua liked this and chuckled to imagine a walk to outwit everything that put paved roads in his path. A long walk. And the longest walk never a man took'll take strength. Oh, yes, a man, a man needs the strength of a young blood, him. Strength in the blood. He thought about the blood of the yard-boss and the boy with the bad face. Joshua leaned on the trailer frame and rocked in his brogans, the whiskey bottle tucked forgotten against his chest, until his stomach felt weak and he stopped. He fished an aspirin tin out his overalls, shook the dust in it into his mouth and washed it down with a swallow from the bottle he did not recall opening.

The sign on the door of Punk's Tavern was lettered in Cherokee and English:

Osiyo-Welcome

And below that: BEER, ICE, HOMEMADE BAR-B-Q.

Joshua, grinning, panting, trembling, put his hand on the sign he had painted for Punk a dozen years before and pushed his way inside. Four men were drinking beer from cans around the pool table in the back, and Punk was telling a red-haired girl at the bar that he hadn't seen her beau since the night two weeks ago when he fought that gas-field goon over when Hank Williams died.

Joshua shook his wet overalls loose from his legs and slung the shoes tied around his neck onto the bar. The girl wrinkled her nose and moved away, and he said, "You got any a him bust-skull, Punk?"

The girl stopped by the jukebox at the end of the bar, dropped a coin in, and Punk said to Joshua, "Kinda beer you say?"

The tom-tom beat of Hank Williams' "Kaw-Liga" throbbed from the jukebox. Joshua held himself up with both forearms on the bar. "Dammit," he whispered beneath the music. "Don't, Punk. I need me some a him real drink, dammit."

Punk put a quart of beer and a Dixie cup in front of Joshua and walked to the jukebox, wiping his hands on a red bar rag. He said something to the girl, slid his arm across her shoulders. She tossed it off and left the tavern, her purse tight against her side. Punk wiped a few tables and came back to the bar with empty beer bottles in each hand.

"Dumb little twat," Punk said, relaxing his belly and putting the empties in a box. "Don't know a good thing when she sees it."

"Punk," Joshua said, sliding his Dixie cup across the bar. "Please, dammit."

Punk held the cup hidden behind the bar, poured in three fingers of clear whiskey from a fruit jar, and set it in front of Joshua, but he didn't turn it loose.

"You know you got no credit here, don'tcha, Josh?"

Joshua slapped his wadded, pink check on the bar. In his blurred vision, the check's shadowed creases were a bramble of thorns.

"Gimme you pen," he said.

Punk unclipped a ballpoint and laid it on the bar. He said, "Put your shoes on, Josh," and watched Joshua tremble through his signature, then looked at the sum on the check.

"A pink un, huh? They turn you out too, Josh?"

"Quit," Joshua said. He drained the Dixie cup.

37

Punk filled the cup again from the Mason jar under the bar.

"You want me to just tell you when this check's drunk up?"

Joshua nodded into the cup, and Punk slammed the cash drawer shut.

Joshua had another then switched to beer and spent an hour drinking it in that busy void where drunkards go.

The tavern began to fill. Punk left the men shooting pool and went behind the bar to turn on an oscillating fan that shook and nicked against its cage.

Joshua had been sitting uncomfortably for what seemed—no, must have been—a long time: his cup was limp and empty, and there were two empty beer quarts at his elbow. And why did his stomach cringe the way it did when Papa John's voice was big and full and cut through him to the cadence of a small Bible slapped against his palm, its cutting worse than the locust switch across his legs? Each slap of the book fell on Joshua fraught with guilt, and Papa John spoke louder and faster as the fan gathered speed, until the slaps and deprecation rained down like lead through a shot-tower sieve. And each slash of the switch cut away some pain. Joshua stood from the bar stool. If there was just a way to get right to the switch, it wouldn't have been so bad. The pain, he realized, was the beer gone through him, so he slipped like a wraith along the wall and out the back door to the privy between the tavern and Punk's trailer house.

Humidity had thickened the air all day, and now low clouds were rolling up a fog at dusk. The moon was a dim sliver bedded in the fog, and a queer yellow light, like the one on nights before a cyclone, held everything close to the earth, making it real and sudden as a lucid hangover does. Joshua squinted to keep it away. When he opened his eyes at the privy door, its knob floated there on a black inch of space. He pushed the door back with his toe. There was no bulb in the socket on the privy wall. Fog filled the space and turned its dark to shapes: a big man, a little man, a man nailed to a tree. Joshua wheeled away, leaned against the side of the privy, and pissed on the ground. It was as bad as the time in Tulsa when a copperhead crawled out of a faucet in the Conoco restroom where he puked.

Joshua did not recall what Punk had done to make him mad, but the things crawling at the edges of his vision made it worse. The drink he had been pounding the bar for finally came and he said between swallows, "God. 'M sorry. Punk."

He got another quart of beer, drank it, and ordered another. Joshua felt sober for the first time that day. He had never gotten over how fast it happened when he drank himself sober, how easy the shakes went away. He unwrapped his crooked, deliberate hand from the fresh Dixie cup, looked down, and began putting his shoes on their proper feet, not easy with the room canted at its crazy angle.

Someone's toe nudged his shoulder.

"C'mon. Get up now, you hear. Punk'll throw your ass out a here ifn you don't get up."

Joshua stood with an icy sweat breaking out on his face.

"'M all right," he said. "Fixin' my shoe." He held a brogan in his hand for the farmer sitting next to him to see. Joshua sat staring at the shoe until it came to him to cross his leg and put it on.

"You all right, Josh?" Punk said. "Look kinda peakéd to me."

"Need me some bite to eat, Punk. You got him eggs?"

Punk brought him a boiled egg on a napkin. Joshua knew at once the he could not peel it, that Punk would offer to, and he said, "Make it a pickled one, Punk, and some jerky."

Joshua set the jerky to soak in a cup of beer and sniffed the strong egg.

"You know, Punk," he said, "they's some people when they gets to drinkin' won't take care a theyself, won't eat nor nothing. Drinkin's not so bad ifn you eat."

Joshua took out the strip of jerky and sucked it. The beer in the jerky was sweet as warm bread dough to him.

"I've heard it called that, liquid bread," Punk said, and Joshua realized he had said something aloud.

Punk shook his head. "How old you, Josh? Must be near forty. You oughta have you a woman to see you eat right."

Joshua said, "Mama's cookin' for me most times now, Punk." But he knew that tonight Papa John would have already made Mama put supper away.

"Didn't know the old man had let you back, Josh. Anyhow, you know what I mean."

"Shit, I got no lead left in my pencil, Punk."

But Punk had turned away, and Joshua did not know whether he had taken the joke or not. "Punk," he said, "ain't I good with cows?"

"Stump broke ones," someone said, and Joshua turned and saw the pock-marked boy from the auction barn swaggering up to the bar.

Joshua gripped the shoulder of the farmer at the bar next to him. "You know me, Punk," he said, as his hand began to slip. "You tell 'em."

The farmer pushed Joshua's hand off and moved to an empty stool down the bar.

"Yeah," said the lanky boy, paying for his beer. "Tell us a good un, Punk."

"I 'member that time you beat Buster Fenno's beef calf to death behind Councilor Godchaux's office," Punk began.

No one ever knew how the calf had strayed into town, and Joshua was not exactly lost that night he cornered it by accident in the blind alley off the square, but he did not know how he got there. He later swore that the unpolled yearling white-face had set upon him there. What he had seen, however, was a parched spirit face welling up out of the dark, wild-eyed and horned as Old Nick. For all its vividness, Joshua would not believe it real; for all his conviction, he could not make it fade. No, he would not believe it. A real thing like that was impossible. A real thing like that would be the Devil himself, powerful and evil. In those first confusing seconds, Joshua had an inkling that what he saw—believed he saw—was inside his eyes, not without. If he could kill it, it was not real. And if the Devil were not real, he could tell Papa John neither was his God. Even when his knuckles collapsed against the hard skull and he had beaten a bloodied brick-bat into powder on it, something would not let him stop.

"Yeah," Punk said, "ol' Josh here broke both his hands, all right. That calf, he beat his brains out on 'em. That were a goodern, Josh."

Joshua had braced his forehead against the bar. "I know how to handle him cows," he said.

"Lots a them him-cows where you come from, Chief?" The boy put his head down on the bar and looked Joshua in the eye.

"Lots a them him-steers down here."

"Makes you feel right at home, don't it?" the boy said, setting his beer on the bar as he straightened up.

Punk told them to stop and started from behind the bar. "Hold on now," he said. "Be Christian."

"Joshua Look'glass," someone called from deep in a smoky booth across the tavern, "s'prised to see you still alive."

"And I ain't no chief, son."

"Son? My mama's white, Chief."

Joshua came off his stool rolling his shoulders; the boy set his feet and cocked a fist; Punk wedged himself between them.

"All right now," Punk said. "That's enough." He turned to the boy. "C'mon, young fella. Let's get something to cool you down."

A hand clasped Joshua's shoulder from behind, pulling him back onto the bar stool. The man had on a shirt with mother-of-pearl buttons, a steel cap on one tooth, and Joshua did not recognize him.

Damn good to see you, Joshua," the man said. "Let me buy you a beer?"

41

"Sure," Joshua said. He looked around and saw Punk at the other end of the bar pouring a shot of bust-skull for the boy with the bad face. And he's probably not got to pay for it neither, Joshua thought. He was sick to have let first the yard-boss and now this boy buffalo him.

"We all got to pay for our tran'gressions, Joshua," the man said. "We cain't get away from knowing our own guilt and deprav'ty."

Joshua recalled him now, the half-breed whiskey preacher called Deacon Gay. "Sure," he said. "Forget it. That's right." He split the pickled egg and rolled its yolk out on the napkin. The brine had turned it the purple of a deep bruise.

Punk set up beers for Joshua and Deacon Gay, then went to pour another shot of the moonshine for the boy glowering at the other end of the bar.

"Forgiveness is fine, Joshua," Deacon Gay was saying, "and times in places like these do try a Christian virtue, but you just makin' drunk talk, Joshua. You got to buck up. You sucked on that bottle 'til now it's startin' to drink from you, brother."

Joshua did not like Deacon Gay, but what the man was saying made some sense to him. He had lately begun to wonder whether drink might be behind his failing sight and resolution, his impotence that would not respond even to masturbation. Joshua pushed his beer away. Deacon Gay was still talking, but Joshua could no longer parse the words. He rode above them, above his anger and the ditch of drunkenness he had slipped into. How clear things had become. Wasn't he a man, and a big man too? His eyes fixed on the boiled eggs stacked in a gallon jar of murky water on the back bar beside the jerky display. A man's the hen to the egg of himself, he thought, and pips hisself forth by main strength.

Deacon Gay's voice broke through. "No, Joshua, there's no strength in a man but it comes from the Lord. You a Christian, ain't you, Joshua?"

The room screamed into focus again, and with it the slap of Papa John's imprecations. Full of himself, Joshua turned on Deacon Gay. "Goddamn you, Deacon Gay. Goddamn you Christian. I'd be arything, be a goddamn Cherokee religion, 'for I'd be him Christian. See what's done my stepdaddy, ain't you? He's a big man when I's little, Deacon Gay. He's a giant then. You seen him. He's drought corn now, all husk and cob. That's crazy religion, Deacon, suck up all a man grit and kernel like him coon emptyin an egg."

Deacon Gay threw his head back and sucked his steel tooth, then picked up both beers and stalked back to his booth.

"Josh," Punk said, gesturing with his thumb, "that fella down there says he's gonna teach you how to use a hotshot. Maybe it's time you mosey on."

"I got credit still, Punk?"

"Yeah. Some."

"Gimme some snort."

Joshua had the drink and after a minute tied his shoes.

"What you think you kin show me?" he said to the boy.

"You wanta come outside?"

"Sure."

Outside, the eerie light was more intense now that the sun had fully set. In it, the fog was palpable—countless bright particles that streamed like a well-head's flame off the back of the boy's hat as Joshua followed him across the gravel parking lot. The boy opened the steel tool box spanning the bed of his pickup and took out two cattle prods.

"I was hoping I'd find you, Chief," the boy said. "You set?"

"Sure," Joshua said. He caught the cattle prod the boy tossed to him.

A half-dozen men, including Punk and Deacon Gay, came out of the tavern to watch the fight and stood lined against the wall by the door. Joshua searched among their faces for encouragement. The yellow light refracted through the fog made their shapes vague to him, lambent as tongues of flame.

Joshua shifted his grip, looked to find the switch on the prod, and the boy gouged beneath his chin, the hot prongs snapping Joshua's head back, slinging a crown of sweat from the ends of his hair.

The boy danced away, aping a fencer's stance. "You pretty good with cows, ain't you, Chief?" he said and lunged for Joshua's face.

Joshua flinched away and brought the battery end of the prod over his shoulder like a splitting maul. It drove the boy's hat down to his ears and the boy to his knees. Then Joshua kicked him. The boy stiffened and toppled back over his boot heels, two jets of blood spouting from a broken nose.

"All right, Josh," Punk shouted. "That's enough."

Deacon Gay said, "God Almighty," drank his beer dry and threw the bottle at Joshua. "Not fair, you heath'n Look'glass."

The bottle landed unbroken in the gravel behind Joshua. He didn't recall anything said about fair. He turned and dropped the cattle prod. Punk and Deacon Gay were coming toward him at a run. Tracers of burning fog whipped from their arms and heads. Joshua crouched, bolted into the woods behind the parking lot, and ran up the hollow away from Punk's until he topped the ridge that would take him home.

Joshua came to the fallen barbed-wire fence that bound Papa John's barren quarter-section. Panting, he threw his arms around a scaled postoak and heard something heavy in his pocket thunk against it.

A numb, spinning minute passed. Joshua turned his back against the tree and slipped the flat whiskey bottle out of his overalls. One swallow left. He hugged the slim oak with his free hand to help keep down his rising gorge. The bad spell passed and he drank and felt better—as best he could. He still said fair don't count. Nobody said anything about fair. That was one thing he ought have no guilt for. No—but sin? No guilt, no sin. But if he had killed that boy . . . It mattered whether he was wrong.

Joshua reeled across the dry pasture, shattered the empty bottle on the flints. He was biggest, boss now. Man, not boy. Damn him, no. But if he was wrong? The switch cut away the shame, cut it away. Sure.

Joshua halted within sight of the unpainted wooden house. He took out his pocket knife and in the static yellow light saw his distorted reflection on the castrating blade marked "For Flesh Only." He could hedge against his being wrong. He could cut away sin himself. He unsnapped the bib of his overalls and let it fall over his belly. He looked closely at the blade, pressed the flat of it against his chest, but could not, could not bring blood. His hand began to shake.

Damn him. He threw the knife on the ground. He was biggest. He didn't need that now.

The window panes in all three rooms rattled and Mama started in her chair when Joshua threw open the door. Mama held her sewing in the light of a tensor lamp set on the cold wood-stove, her worried face grained and brown as oiled walnut.

"Joshua, hush," she said. "You going to wake Mister John."

"Damn him," Joshua said. He slumped defiantly into Papa John's rocking chair. "I'm biggest, Mama. I'm boss now."

Papa John was a small, stooped man with sharp bones close beneath his brittle hide. He wore bifocals and a long shirt buttoned to the collar. In his hands was an old-fashion .22 pump, a relic from some carnival, all its riflings shot out. Mama was praying, "Lord, don't let they be nothing wrong." As he stepped from the door of his bedroom, Papa John lowered the hammer with his thumb.

He did not raise his voice. "Get out of my chair, Joshua, and go to bed," he said.

Joshua gripped the arms of the chair and rocked harder, staring at the cold stove. Where's my supper?" he said.

Papa John leaned the rifle against the door jamb, went onto his bedroom, and returned with a thick locust switch.

"Get out of my chair and go to bed, Joshua," he said.

"I'm biggest. I'm boss now."

Papa John lashed across Joshua's face, leaving an angry welt on his cheek. "Honor thy father and thy mother," Papa John said and swung the switch again.

Joshua wrenched it from the old man's hand. "I'm boss now," he said and snapped the switch in two. He could hear Mama sobbing prayers from the dark corner she had moved to.

Papa John had the gun in his hands. "You are leaving my house, Joshua," he said.

"You not gonna make me, Papa John." Joshua stood from the chair.

Papa John shot him in each leg.

Joshua fell back in the chair, splitting the caned bottom. He was dazed, incredulous. He had always heard a shooting didn't hurt. "Can't make me," he said through clenched teeth.

Papa John shot him again, the weak slug traveling around Joshua's ribs and lodging in the small of his back.

Pain passed beyond all thought of sin or guilt. "Wait, Papa," Joshua said, as if begging a moment to compose himself. He held his long hands in front of him, palms out. A tumbling round keyholed through one palm and buried in his belly just below the ribs. Joshua looked at Papa John through his fingers. He felt something inside of him let go, pain blossom sudden as milkweed. "Wait, Papa," he said. "I had enough now, Papa."

The Widening Gyre

They still come to Indian Territory, the luckless, the desperadoes, the drifters. They blow in here wild and harsh and desperate to be spent as dust devils whipping the capstan stench off Boz Stratton's gas field on a hot August noon. Those little cyclones that do make it this far ride themselves to earth on our wooded ridges that divide Little Dixie from the plains, this land so often wrongly surveyed that it once appeared on maps to be in three counties. But always it has been the terminus for dust-devils and drifters who, like the sedentary dust we all are, are made mad by their unwilled movement and intuit it—intuit it because they believe they are only simple people rushing intent and hungry to what they think is a simple place. Their motive force? Time, and their fear of it, of being consumed, flashing from crack of black to back again without leaving a single spark behind. They whirl through here as though their grim velocity could escape itself, obliterate motion, and they thrill me with the same pity and loathing I knew when my setter bitch swallowed a treble fish hook and ripped out her litter trying to kill the pain.

Those were my thoughts—morbid, inchoate, bereft—as I looked down on the square from my office window and saw a girl carrying a roped suitcase drag her gaunt little daughter off the Grayhound in front of the post office. For a moment, she seemed to sort so well with the images I was conjuring that I thought she was one of them, had walked out of my thoughts. Her dark hair was lacquered stiff, impervious to the hot wind; her white jeans tight, bi-lunar, shapely, not impervious to wistful lechery that soured quickly: eighteen pushing forty-five, and I had work to do.

47

Buster Fenno, forty-some-odd and looking older, was with her coming out of the Red Horse Lounge when I crossed the square later that afternoon on my way to the courthouse. I wondered whether his dairy herd would miss their evening milking. Buster had the roped suitcase in his hand and the little girl, one fist clapped to a cleft ear, on his shoulder. I doubt that Buster has any particular insight into the minds of children, but he does indulge them. I've handled both his divorces, and what each woman held against him boiled down to the fact that Buster wouldn't make the kids mind and spent too many nights listening to his hounds run the sly coyotes that folks out here call wolves. I watched the fierce, skittish young woman nuzzle Buster and felt a little sorry for him. Her name, I learned, was Lee Ann.

I saw her on the square from time to time, parking Buster's Dodge flatbed, going into the Red Horse at noon. The child was seldom with her. Nights when a widower's insomnia kept me out late on the porch swing, I sometimes saw her cruising out of town past my house with one of the roughnecks from Stratton's gas field. And they drew in their wake that reek of capstan and kerosene. Yes, she was harsh and as fast a baggage as you'll ever see, vulnerable to most any counterfeit of warmth, any bootleg of affection.

Still, the recurrent motion of clocks has cured me of even less than it ever could Lee Ann. Memory of my wife is a deep bruise on these old bones, and old bones are slow to mend. After a night tossed by those memories, I was awake before dawn, despondent and unrested, so I dressed and drove east into the hills to wait for morning and, I suppose, to put movement and distance between me and my desolate four-poster bed.

Seconds crawled across the face of my watch. I hoped I might spot game feeding in the rising light, but there is little here. The deer and turkey were hunted to near-extinction by the lumber crews decades ago, and the second-growth timber is yet sparse and stunted, poor habitat. So I lingered in the rising light, waiting for the

Courthouse Cafe to open at six. When I circled the square at a quarter-of, I found Lee Ann lying disheveled on the liars' bench outside my street level door.

As I shook her awake, she raised one knee, letting her skirt ride up to expose the black down that marked the razor line on her thigh. I got her to stand and looked around the empty square. A window shade in the cafe fluttered and shot up. I unlocked my door and helped her up the stairs.

"You're a nice man," she kept saying, her breath thick with whiskey. "I remember you. A nice man, you know that?"

I led her into the small conference room off my office and felt a peculiar unease as she toed her shoes off and sprawled face down on the sofa, my pity deep as grief.

"Where do you remember me?" I said.

"Alla time. I seen you alla time. Nice straight old man with the hat and brisket and tie."

"Brisket? You mean my vest?"

"Mmm." She arched the lean whip of her back, rolled that puffed face toward me, and reached to run a chipped nail along my gold watch chain. "Yes. Nice vest-brisket man."

"Exactly what," I said, pulse clotting in my throat, "were you doing down there? On the bench?"

She balled her hands beneath her chin and turned her mouth into a pout that made her face look limp and used. "That guy, that bastard man. He was afraid to take me home. Who's afraid of Daddy Buster? Was gonna take me to Tulsa, he said, but he didn't have no map. Not all he didn't have."

Then her eyes snapped me into focus and all the fierceness I had sensed before was there again. "He'll take me today. You'll see. He will."

"Will he? Why is that?"

She pressed her face into the cushion and mumbled, "Unzip

49

me, nice man."

"Get some sleep," I said, then turned and left the room.

I sat in my office wondering whether I would have taken her at twenty? At forty? No, although I might have wished it, and either way would lead to regret.

I held no brief on what I felt, knew no precedent to give form and meaning to my pity and vague desire. Was it because she quickened urges that I have ever held in check by reverence for memory and a faith in the rectitude of order. She possessed no such memory, had lost it in a motion fleeing time and lived her life with tragic, neurotic intensity. Why then that fearful attraction? Because now in the second year after my Irene's death memory still pressed her close and tossed my sleep with her, and Lee Ann's motion stood for the freedom one has when age forgets youth and sin trumps shame?

Still, it is memory that, like the wolf hound's scar, affirms and records us, Guess County. Such as it is, it still stands for duration and the fact that we have husbanded the dust. And by its cultivation wouldn't I somehow survive even the memory I left behind? Procreation's not just of the flesh; I wished the children I've never had to know that. There is no profit in wholly being, in living Lee Ann's intensity, and never knowing from where you've come, though that history be but a chronicle of pain. Is memory worth no more than the pain it obtains? If I lay with her would it give me pain? And desire surcease? Would it make me whole?

I went to the cafe. Over breakfast I read all the papers, even the insipid cartoons, and when I returned to the office, she was gone. But the air conditioner that I had failed to turn on moaned softly. The blinds had been raised, and morning light sifted pale and warm across my desk where six newly sharpened yellow pencils lay in a row on a pad of legal foolscap. On it was a note written in a looping school-girl hand:

Nice vest brisket man—
I waited and waited but you never come
back to unzip me tho I want you to know
'm obliged. I like you a lot I relly do and
youll see he will take me he relly will.
You only feel like your bettern me cause
your such a bleeder but youll see you dont
have to cause I never will be the one bleedin
again like that.
Thanks anyways.

L.A.

If I were a more insightful man, perhaps I would not have wondered what that note intended. Perhaps I would have forgotten her. But all talk runs to gossip in a small town, and I heard things I'd as soon not: that she had move in with Buster the same day I first saw them together; that he indulged her the way he had his kids (although he claimed she "wived" him as well); that the rust-seamed trailer he lived in on his small dairy farm was where Lou Ann left her little daughter every day she was in the Red Horse; that at night Buster made a pallet on the bed of the Dodge and took the child with him to listen to his bugle-throated hounds run wolves.

Later that week I saw them quarreling on the street—her at least. Buster is as placid as his cows. And the more deferential he became, the softer the word he used, the more furious she became. She trembled on the cusp of fury, waiting for his own anger to break over her.

"Hit me. Go ahead. Aren't you going to hit me?" She squinted and raised her chin to one side in a practiced movement.

They were outside the drugstore. The bony little girl was in Buster's arms, fist to ear, trying to hide in his collar.

"No, honey. Uh-uh. I don't want to do nothing like that."

51

"Then don't you try to tell me how to raise my child, you hear? Hear? You can just keep her then." She spun and walked away toward the beauty parlor.

I stepped beside Buster and watched her hips twitch. I felt somehow complicit, obliged to make Buster feel good.

"'Day, Mr. Fenno. Mighty fond of those babies, aren't you?" I tried to chuck the little girl under the chin. She turned her head, exposing the split, red ear. It was not an old scar. Her diaper smelled and was dampening Buster's shirt.

"Sure, Couns'lor. You know, I used to have a three-bedroom house. I's a good man before then. Sure, I like kids."

"Starting a new family?"

"Not with that one, Couns'lor. That one ain't never goin to have no brand. Nor mine nor nobody's. God willin'."

When the events of the rest of that day led to the court's appointing me counsel for her defense, I had to recuse myself, less for any conflict of interest than for the conflict of my emotions. Not that that was how I put it to the judge. Still, I found myself making efforts to find out more than even a counsel needs to know. I saw her mother and some other relatives in Texas, talked to the roughneck who didn't take her to Tulsa, and to Buster, of course. I learned a lot from what she later told me in exchange for cigarettes and gum. From all that and some that I've surmised, this is what I know.

Lee Ann never knew her father. He died before she was born, but she said she always wanted one. She had an understandable if unhealthy malice toward her mother, a frightened, lard-complexioned woman give to Old Testament invective parsed from sermons at the Assembly of Yahweh she attended. So when she was barely fourteen and her mother married a pint-and-Bible lay preacher from the church, Lee Ann wanted him to want her. And he did. And he had her, again and again, although Lee Ann could no longer recall the first time.

She hadn't even been sure what to call what they did.

Penance, he said, for sins, grace, divine satisfaction.

Fearful of the wrath of her stepfather's god and shamed by her own complicity, Lee Ann never told whose the still-born baby was. At fifteen, by some fractured logic of her own, she knew that no one but her own child could ever love her again. She could accept, almost welcome, her mother's scorn and hysteria of shame, but finally she could not bear it. She met a trucker in a place called the Big Rig Rest, and he took her away. He became the father of Tammi, the little cleft-eared girl, and he loved Lee Ann until she started to show. He left her at a truck stop in Needles, and she began sleeper-hopping back to Texas, filled with vague guilt and incredulity and a hunger for warmth. She longed for that perfect, loving child and feared the depraved cells multiplying in her womb, bursting her jeans.

Her trip home took six days that seemed all like night to her—delirious amphetamine nights, carry-out meals in the fusty sleeper-cabs of Macks and White Freightliners. All the rigs were on short hauls, she said, and all the drivers said it would be all right. They would find her another hop. *Lie back; it's going to be all right.* Around Albuquerque they still tell of her circling town all one night in four different trucks. She thought each one was taking her closer to home.

Tammi was born a month premature. A pitifully thin child, she was never anything else. Lee Ann was terrified she might die, might die and waste her shame and her only chance to be loved. Her feelings about the baby were mixed and, finally, irreconcilable. She had to love the child, she thought, in order to be loved, yet guilt corroded affection. And the child was ugly: thin, slack mouthed, almond eyed. Lee Ann's unmet yearnings drove he to men who could not love the child. It is strange to me that she should have expected as much unalloyed affection from Tammi as she later did stern husbandry from Buster, for he would be no more capable of returning her hate than the baby was capable of returning the love Lee Ann had only an imagining of.

Lee Ann and her mother were alone again then. The stepfather was gone, fled to Del Rio to found a radio mission. They listened for him, but he never made the air. Her mother brought home pamphlets from the church, screeds on the maggot of God consuming corrupted flesh. They galvanized Lee Ann's guilt, made it an obstacle to the meager pleasures she found in the motel rooms and backseats of salesmen's cars. But benzedrine, and the whiskey she used to kill it, leveled the guilt. She fought with her mother. They lived off church baskets and food stamps. Neither could hold a job. Most nights, Tammi was left with her fretful, glossolaliac Gram.

The three nights a week her mother attended church, Lee Ann took the baby with her to laundromats and bars, hoping to ingratiate herself with someone who would look after Tammi "for a few minutes" while she sought with older, anonymous men the solace the baby was supposed to provide. Several nights, strangers brought the baby home, and one night the police. A social worker came to call. This all fueled the fights Lee Ann and her mother had. They were wild, unfair fights, filled with tears and accusations, and sometimes ended with whippings for the child who cried often at first. "Though," Lee Ann told me, "eventually she got to be well behaved."

One Friday night, a drunk, peroxided woman arrived at the house with Tammi and two Mexican men. One of them had his shirt off. Lee Ann's mother was terrified. They wanted Lee Ann to go to a party with them. Lee Ann's mother took Tammi, latched the screen, and said she wasn't home. Lee Ann wobbled out of a new Buick with three men in it in front of the house the next Sunday at dark. Her stiff hair was crushed in back and her short skirt twisted to one side. But except for the discomfort of walking, she was mercifully free of pain for a while, free of the demands of a frail child and her mother's imprecations and that vulnerable yearning of her own now numb flesh.

She wedged herself diagonally in the jamb of the open kitchen door, oozing musk and alcohol. Her mother, at the kitchen table clinching a chipped tea cup in bent hands—the very cup she served me coffee in when she told of it—did not look up, looked into the trembling cup and asked flatly, "Do you know who brought your baby home?"

Shame broke across Lee Ann as sharp as a slap, shame she hated the more for feeling she deserved it. And it was all for Tammi. She locked herself in the room she and the baby shared and snapped on the light.

Tammi stood shakily, fumbling at the bars of her crib. She was always thirsty. She began to cry for water.

Lee Ann tried to silence her, caught clumsily at the baby's lips to pinch off the dry sobs. Tammi howled. Lee Ann dragged her to her chest, patted her clumsily, covered her mouth with one hand, made rough motions to comfort the wailing child. She walked the floor of the hot little room and Tammi began to cry louder and her mother's voice rose and fell in execration.

"You are an abomination before the Lord, Lee Ann."

"Stop it, Mama. Stop it. You started it all."

"One abomination before the Lord."

"You gave me to him," Lee Ann screamed, meaning the whiskey preacher, "so's he wouldn't be pestering you."

Her mother keened and hammered the steel table top with her fists.

Tammi flailed at Lee Ann's neck. A string of glass beads snapped and rattled on the bare linoleum. Lee Ann knelt for them and the room began to swim. She stood, twisting to catch it.

"Look what you done," she said, spinning. "Look what you done."

Lee Ann spun wildly, but not wildly enough not to feel herself caving in, collapsing into solitary helplessness. The bars of the crib flicked by. There was a crack, silence, and she was unconscious on the rag rug beside her bed.

The next morning, her mother had to wet the crib sheet to loosen the dried blood pasting it to the baby's head. Tammi had a deep gash in one ear, the ear Lee Ann did not take time to have basted before she took Tammi and left that place for an easier one.

Buster had already loaded the baby in his truck and taken her back to his trailer, where she would sit alone while he tended his chores, when I looked out my office window at a ragged dust devil scattering itself on the gritty sidewalks around the square as Lee Ann came out of the beauty parlor. She turned and faced the plate glass window, glaring past her lettered reflection at the half dozen local women inside. They had put her through a shunning, pretended they were alone and said what they thought of her, none of it kind. Lee Ann told herself they were jealous of her, jealous because she wasn't like them, wasn't going to marry Buster Fenno, was eighteen and didn't sag and didn't wear a bra. She began teasing her lacquered hair higher with the spike of a rat-tail comb. She put the comb away and swayed across the sun-soft asphalt toward the Red Horse Lounge, swinging a clutchpurse stiffly away from her hips. A pain like hunger ground in her stomach.

She was hurrying to meet her gas-field roughneck in the Red Horse for lunch—a fact that the ladies in the beauty parlor seemed to have known—the lothario who was taking her to Tulsa.

A loud, overworked evaporative cooler rolled wet air around inside the Red Horse Lounge. The plastic booth she slid into clung damply to her clothes. She felt her hair to see whether it was wilting, bought a beer, looked at the watch Buster had given her, and wondered where her man was. She hoped Buster would bring milk for Tammi back from the dairy barn, milk she should have bought with the money she spent in the beauty parlor getting ready for her trip to Tulsa. She damned Buster for believing that unpasteurized milk caused disease. The beer seemed to calm her gnawing stomach, so she bought another.

The waitress asked whether she wanted a sandwich, and Lee Ann said she was waiting on someone, thank you.

The bar began to fill with men, mostly farmers who had brought their stock to auction and their wives to the beauty shop. The younger men eyed her, but no gas-field roughneck. She had five dollars left. She thought about the baby in the baking trailer. She ordered another beer. She would drink it and maybe one more, and if the sonofabitch didn't show, she was gone. She would still have enough left to buy milk. She wondered who else besides those biddies in the beauty parlor knew he was meeting her here. She looked at the weathered farmers laughing with the waitress, the lean and randy boys. Did they? Yes. They all knew. She knew they did. That sonofabitch had done this on purpose.

The conviction that all of Gist had conspired to humiliate her swallowed Lee Ann. But Tammi, Tammi really cared. Tammi was Lee Ann's love and comfort. She drank two beers straight from the bottle and swayed through the wet air out of the Red Horse into the blistering heat, feeling every eye on her spine.

The heat held her back against the door of the bar, a slow twist of early vertigo rising from her belly, a feeling as though she had swallowed tobacco, as though she were quick with another early, alien life. She turned toward the Co-op grocery by the feed mill, brushing the hot brick facades of the stores around the square with one hand the way a bedded drunk holds one foot to the floor to still his whirling, incomprehensible room.

When she reached the store, her clothes were sopped with sweat, her tongue grit dry. She opened the quart of milk she bought and drank half of it before she went back out, dreading the idea of having to walk back to Buster's trailer.

The roughneck drove by as she stepped into the street. She saw him look at her with only bare recognition in his smile. He smiled and drove on without even slowing. Lee Ann stood stunned by her anger and humiliation. She wadded the top of the limp paper sack in her fist and faced away, stiff with rage, to meet a debris-filled dust devil swirling around one lobe of the feed mill's quadrefoil silo. She slapped at the chaff and shook a lock of lacquered hair into her face. She fought the urge to bawl, thought of Tammi wanting to touch her pretty hair. She smelled her own sweat, and it was larger than her body. She felt dirty, exposed, and pregnant. She wanted to be held.

Meanwhile, my day had run to frustration with a title search, and I took myself to the Red Horse for a rare afternoon beer. The place was emptying as I came in. The last of the flushed farmers edged past me at the door, nodding and calling me by name. I took the stool nearest the cash register and tried to hold my aching back erect.

Was I a bleeder, as she had called me? Or was she cunning enough to hope my denying it would drive me toward her? Even then I sensed clearly her attraction to surrogate daddies, so perhaps my pity was my way of keeping her at arm's length. But would loving save her? Mine? Anyone's? My own loneliness widened like ripples in the heavy air. I was rapt by a depressing fear that it was that loneliness which ruled me. But at the same time, the notion that I could, even in my aged grief, be a bond to hold us both from falling alone back into the clockwise dust's grand design welled up a sense of purpose—when Buster Fenno came blinking into the dim tavern. He guided along the bar straight toward me.

"Couns'lor," he said, "we got to have words."

Buster was in a powerful state, and strong emotions in a man not suited to them are easily misconstrued. I read grief for rage and felt a fool for not having told him of the morning I'd spent with Lee Ann. Buster, I thought, was bent on some grotesque point of honor.

"I think I can explain this, Mr. Fenno."

"What the hell *explain*, Couns'lor," he almost wailed, and it was then I saw his inexplicable grief. "I just come from what she done, Couns'lor. God, she said she's kill herself ifn they tried to take her before you come."

And he told me what she had done, and later so did she.

The trailer's dull skin shimmered in the heat like rippling foil, and inside a single oscillating fan moved the air sluggishly. Tammi sat at the counter separating the living room and kitchen, wearing only a wet diaper and picking dry cereal from a bowl. A silent image rolled methodically down the television screen. Tammi looked up from it when Lee Ann walked in.

"Thirsty, Mama," she said. "Thirsty."

Lee Ann's stomach began to boil. "Here's some milk, baby," she said and reeled down the corridor to the bathroom. She washed her face and kept from being sick by pressing her cheek to her cheek in the mirror. Sobbing, she began to tease furiously at her shredded hair. She flicked the chaff out with the tail of the comb and tried to lick loose ends into place. She was silently damning the world when she heard the clatter and Tammi begin to cry. Lee Ann willed everything to stop—her humiliation, her tears, her crying child. She shut her eyes and held the comb between her breasts with both hands.

Tammi bawled.

Lee Ann cracked her temple on the door as she jerked it open and stumbled into the hall. Banking off walls, she went to one knee on the living room carpet. Tammi sprawled splay-legged on the floor, screaming, holding her ear. Cereal and the warm, faintly blue milk blotted the carpet around her.

On her knees, Lee Ann struggled closer, hissing, "See. See. Now see what you done. Shut that crying. Shut it if you love me. Don't you? Don't you?"

She slapped at the baby's mouth and, forgetting the comb in her hand, scored her deeply on the throat with its tail. A welt of bright blood brimmed the cut and spread down Tammi's chest. She shrieked in terror and threw herself on her face. Lee Ann went rigid. Through the sweat falling in her eyes, she saw the rent ear and the fresh blood appear to multiply and cover her frail, disfigured child. Aghast at what she saw and in order to get rid of it, she stabbed Tammi again and again with the tang of the comb without remembering any one time alone.

"Don't you ever run from me. Don't you cry. Don't you. Don't you love me? Say it. Please. Say you do."

When the sheriff and the ambulance had gone, Buster and I walked silently back to his truck. I listened to the lowing of his herd, anxious for their milking. Lee Ann hadn't spoken to me when they brought her out, only wanted me there, it seems. A tremor of weariness rippled up my shank as I mounted the cab. I straightened and leaning over the top of the door looked to where the land fell away toward the parched plains. There were specks of abandoned derricks in the distance, heat rising from an earth pitted and emptied by ever more desperate wildcat wells. The heat rose and stirred fine dust, turned it in the gyre of a growing twister.

"Take me home," I said to Buster Fenno, and shut the door.

Singing Convention

Her mother said, "I don't have to explain anything to you, justify anything to you, or listen to any of your silliness. You will not sing that song. Period. End of discussion. Now go up to the spring and get Walter his water."

Twelve-year-old Essie Calico—in Levi's, Puma hightops, and a Coldplay t-shirt—followed the sandstone steps of the path through the trees from the Visitors Center to the top of the mound where a double spring of salt and sweet water flowed from either end of a single cleft in the stone crown. The nearby ridges were steep, rocky, scabbed with flint bluffs, but the slope around the springs had been gentled with earth by the vanished Mound People, whose riverine confederacy, Essie could recite, once stretched from Ohio almost to the Plains, hundreds of years before the Osage roamed here, longer than that before the Cherokee came. It was mild September, green still on the morning-dappled oaks, the air not as thick as summer's, yet still not crisp with fall. Essie scarcely noticed. She kept her head down, eyes on the rising path. She carried an empty gallon jug in each hand, one for salt water and one for sweet, for the opening ceremonies of the pow-wow that evening, to launch the fall tourist season at Tsalagi Traditional Village.

Essie had heard old people say that the eight-foot fissure in the low dome of rock where the springs flowed looked like "a woman's parts," and that there was meaning in salt and sweet water both flowing from it. Her mother said she should always call it "the mouth" of the springs, that the other was a vulgar superstition. Where the

61

smaller salt-spring plumed, gray crystals crusted thick on the blackrock lips. Essie pinched a lump and put it to her tongue. It was metallic, familiar, reminding her, as it always did, of coming here with her grandmother and of her stories about panning salt and making soap, the climax of an autumn ritual: rounding up the hogs set loose to fatten on forest acorns, herding them to the scalding hollow, and sorting them by ear-marks among the families camped there.

The sweet-water spring fed a stream that flowed through the hollow, and worn into the stone bank were nineteen broad, shallow depressions where generations of Cherokee had scalded and rolled and scraped their hogs. When the scalding and scraping were done, they used the iron boiling pots to render the lard for soap. Children carried water from the mound, and women panned its salt to cure the hams and sides of bacon, to give savor to their lives.

What had been a celebration of life's necessity was only a performance now, a going-through-the-motions, her mother said, like Walter Deer-in-water insisting the ceremonial water come from its source, but Essie's imagination took pleasure in it. She entered that other world as readily as she inhabited her Village costume—part buckskin, part satin—rapt by the identification she felt with the old ways when she sang about them, their passing, much as she understood all things better, she thought, when she sang about them. There were free brochures and self-guiding iPods for rent at the Visitors Center, but no guides or docents, so when the reenactors were on break, Essie often took up with tour groups to talk them through the finer points of boiling lye soap or dressing a terrapin for dinner.

She stopped in the cedar brake that screened the back of the Visitors Center and put down her plastic jugs to let her shoulders rest. In the storage area behind the café, Lily, the chubby chef, was arranging pork shoulders and hot links in the smoker, and her fry-cook was assembling the propane grills and fish-fryers that would all be in use tonight. From here, on the lowest bench of the mound, Essie could see the entire Village: the sawtooth palisade on three sides, winding paths lined with replica huts and houses from centuries past—thatch, wattle-and-daub, hewn-log, and dog-trot—where the reenactors feathered arrows, wove baskets, and scraped hides. Salt pans the size of tractor tires were stacked beside the spring-fed creek. In the middle of the Village, the Walkingstick twins, Howard and Harold, stood on ladders adjusting the spotlights in the performance pavilion. They were lithe, taciturn, muscular boys with long hair who, to Essie's disappointment, largely ignored her. She frowned at the nearly flat front of her t-shirt, picked up the water, and walked down to the Village to deliver it to Walter Deer-in-water, Chief Cultural Interpreter and general factotum.

"Mr. D.," Essie said, "*siyo.*"

Deer-in-water, astraddle a hewn-log bench, looked up from the bone trident he was binding to the shaft of an arrow and said, "*Siyo*, Essie. *Tohiju?*"

"I'm good. Where do you want your water?"

Deer-in-water grunted softly and nodded to the ground beside him. He wrapped the strip of bark a final time around the gig and split and laced it in an invisible finish.

"That," Essie said, examining the arrow, "is cool. You can't even see it. Show me how you do that."

Deer-in-water stood and brushed off his khakis. "Last one of those for today," he said. He put the arrow in a wooden quiver with a clutch of others and picked up the two jugs.

"You settled on what you're singing, Essie?"

She fell into step beside him.

"All except the modern. Mom gave me a list of what *she* says is okay."

Deer-in-water grunted noncommitally. He knew about the

63

blow-up between Essie and her mother—everybody with ears knew about *that*.

Two days earlier, during a sound check at the pavilion, Essie began singing a song written by her father, Eddie Fulbright, the one that went to #23 on the Billboard Chart a dozen years ago and, as Deer-in-water recalled, ruined Eddie with its success, turned him grandiose and dissolute. She was just finishing the first reprise of the chorus, the lines everyone remembered, even when they had forgotten the name of the song:

"Patches of beauty sign your name in the wind,

bright diamonds that out-spangle the sun,"

when Addy, her mother, mounted the stage in a fury, breathless from her run down the hill, tears sheeting her cheeks, and began rasping, "Stop it. Stop it. Stop it," until she could at last scream, with her feet planted wide and her arms stiff at her sides, "You will not sing that song. Do you hear me? Do you? You will not sing that song, Esther Jean."

And Essie shouting back, by then also in tears, "No wonder he left you. All you care about's yourself. You hate it because it's good and it's his and you're not either one."

All this with the microphone still on, the amps up, shaking dust from the walls of the mud-daubed huts. Thank goodness, Deer-in-water thought, it was only employees here.

"Essie," he said, "I'll talk to her, if you think it'll help."

"No. Then she'd just be mad at both of us."

"Well, we better get back to our snake-killing, then. I'll see you at family meal."

Essie returned to the Visitors Center determined to be cheerful and helpful, hoping it might move her mother to relent. Other arguments—"I haven't rehearsed anything else." "I can do 'Kites' acappella." "People still remember it."—had not. She opened a cardboard box and began shelving star-patterened jars of "Tsalagi Red

Salt," the clay-colored delicacy and economic backbone of the Calicoes since 1907, when Elias Mouse, her great-great-great grandfather, was granted allotment rights to Double Springs Mound.

"Esther," her mother said from the connecting door to the café, "every year we make, I don't know, probably a thousand times what your great-grandmother ever did off salt, and our reenactors don't pan a tithe of what she did all by herself. It's all because we're adding value for the tourists, sweetheart. We give them what they think they're supposed to want: clay-colored salt. They're our gift, Essie. If the Creator used to send us deer and fish and turkey, now He sends us tourists."

"And ribbon-shirts from Vietnam," Essie said, determined to sound perky. "And don't forget the bingo."

"Huh. Bingo. That's for church and the tribe casinos; god and government got a lock on that. No, we'll leave luck up to them, baby, because what we have is better. Nobody's got a monopoly on traditions. People come here expecting certain things, and there are traditions and there are . . . traditions. So, for six years now people have come to expect—it's become a tradition—for us to have . . . certain kinds of things we do, even in the singing convention."

"When you put the sound system in, and Mr. Tenkiller and Miz Glass didn't want it, you said that traditions have to change or they die."

"Six years isn't old enough to die," her mother said. "And be sure you test those new dolls before you put them out. The kit's in the broom-closet cupboard."

She went back into the café and shut the door behind her.

The dolls were from Haiti and tested lead-free. After she finished arranging them, Essie patrolled the aisles of souvenirs and glass cases of artifacts excavated from the mound, irritably rearranging displays and missing her sister, Patty, who had left for college in August. Patty was on a vocal-music scholarship and had taken two blue ribbons at the singing convention, doing for her modern songs gut-wrenching country ballads of poverty and unrequited love. But unlike Essie, who wanted to invest herself in whatever she sang, Patty was stone-cold about it.

"Little Sis," she'd said just a few days before she left, bobbing to Radiohead and smoothing a water-soluble tattoo on Essie's arm, "Mom's even behind her own times. I mean, "Surrey With the Fringe on Top"? Give me a freaking break. It's all about a great-big smile and whatever crap Mom tells the judges to like."

Last year, her first to compete, Essie won second-place in the junior division, doing the Beatles' "Blackbird." After that, her mother said, "Second? Well, we'll just have to be more careful about what we chose."

We. Frustration rippled Essie's shoulders. *We,* she thought, *aren't singing the song. It's me. And it's* my *dad's song and that's all it's about. About how much she hates him.*

Eddie Fulbright and Adeline Calico—she never used his name and insisted that her daughters keep hers—had been divorced for almost five years, and Essie had seen her father three times since, most recently last Thanksgiving. Her mother had let him stay for an hour, and it was raining, so Essie sat beside him on the couch, loving him and oppressed by his nostalgia—"Hey, Es, you remember those times when we usta . . . ?"— by the falseness of his laugh, by his belt being too long, his smell of stale tobacco and strong cologne. He was different from the father who danced soft-shoe while he fixed breakfast, made Essie and Patty sock monkeys and book shelves, had optimism to fill a room. Singing his song was Essie's way of restoring something of what she loved in her father, giving him back what he'd lost, what her mother had taken from him, from her.

The café and gift shop opened at noon that day, the Village

itself at two, so all the employees gathered at eleven for a common meal from the soup-and-sandwich buffet. Essie sat with her mother and Deer-in-water and a young woman from the Gist *Argus* who was writing the annual feature about the Village pow-wow for the newspaper's Sunday magazine.

She said to Essie, "I understand you're the singer in the family."

"My sister, too," Essie said, "but she's away at school, so I guess it's just me now."

"And what is it you're doing for the talent competition?"

"Singing convention, we usually call it," Addy said. "Except we do give ribbons. And gift certificates. But we want people to associate it with old-time fellowship."

"Ooookay," the reporter said, pretending to scribble in her notebook. "So, what *are* you doing, . . . Esther, isn't it?"

"Essie. Uh-huh."

Essie had aligned the crusts of her sandwich, carefully torn off any lettuce that showed, and was wiping it on her tray.

"Well," she said, ticking off each phrase on the fingers of her clean hand and looking away, "you always do one hymn—usually in Cherokee, but it doesn't have to be—and one traditional song that's always in Cherokee, and then something modern, like a pop song or something."

She hoped that if she avoided the reporter's eyes, she would stop asking questions.

"Really?" The reporter nodded to Essie's t-shirt. "What are you going to sing? 'Lost!'?"

Essie didn't want to talk about this; she wanted to curl onto a knot.

Deer-in-water laughed. "No," he said, "don't think the Tsalagi Traditional Village is quite ready for Coldplay." He looked at Addy. "But we're always expanding our appeal. Aren't we, Miz Calico? So who knows?"

"We're very family-oriented," Addy said. "Traditional family values. You should come back for the show."

Essie tore more lettuce.

"Oh, I'll be there," the reporter said, smiling.

"Good," said Deer-in-water. "Let's eat then. We have to change into costume directly, but I'll be around all afternoon, introduce you to some of the reenactors."

Essie's costume for the afternoon and the first rounds of singing was a pastiche of periods. She wore high, brightly-beaded, fawn moccasins, a buckskin skirt dyed green and trimmed in ribbon fringe, a red satin top with puffy sleeves, lace cuffs, and a tailored waist, and jewelry of glass beads, worked silver, and mussel shells. A white comb of antler and fishbone held her hair in place, and a small flute dangled on a lanyard from her wrist. She turned and looked at herself in the ladies' room full-length mirror and thought she might be getting hips.

Her anger and resentment toward her mother were a little abated, but not her will to do her father's song. She was not, as Addy had charged, being stubborn for stubborn's sake: she could not put in words exactly what she felt, but she knew that, for her, singing his song was important, that it mattered in a way bigger than the Village and its traditions, beyond her mother's spite.

Essie had a role in the Village but no specific job, a little, she thought, like Mickey Mouse at Disneyland, but with a way-cooler costume. Besides standing in for the reenactors when she had the chance, she greeted visitors at the entrance with a cheerful "Welcome, friends."—*Osiyo, tsunali'i.*—wandered the paths answering questions about history and traditions, or sometimes simply stood in a quiet patch of shade and played the five-hole flute. *Ambiance*, her mother called it.

"*Siyo*, Essie."

Outside one of the hewn-log cabins, Harold Walkingstick sat on a stump that he had contoured to make a seat. On a blue blanket beside him were a half-dozen flutes waiting to be finished, and in his hands he held one freshly oiled, a long, seven-hole flute carved from white ash with a bird's-wing pattern in the grain, like a skein of geese flying its length.

"*Siyo*, Harold. Pretty flute."

Walkingstick grunted softly. "This one's got a nice sound. Got a thumb hole for extra notes, too. Give it a try."

Essie giggled as she fumbled to find the right angle for her lips and the spacing for her fingers on the stops, then ran some scales and played the opening bars of "Blackbird."

"Wow," she said, turning the flute in her hands. "This is some whistle, Harold. Pitch is perfect."

He grunted and picked up another.

"Keep that one," he said. "Play it around. Be good advertising."

"Thanks, Harold. *Wado*."

"You're welcome, little sister. And, hey, good luck tonight. And remember to clap loud for Howard."

Just outside the palisade, shielded from the parking lot by a bois d'arc thicket, was the equipment shed. The walls and ceiling of the shed were filled with silver-backed insulation, so no one outside could hear her. Essie sat on the seat of the backhoe tractor, hummed the verse to her father's song, and picked it out on the flute until she could negotiate the octave change at the end. The chorus was easier, only five notes repeated and a bridge back to the verse. She played it until her fingers had it memorized and found herself entering the music much as when she sang. Perhaps because it was his, singing it wasn't necessary to know the swell of love and happiness that every girl who heard it wanted for her own. *And*, she thought as she let the last note die, *who wouldn't?*

She slipped the flute beneath her beaded belt and went back into the Village.

Essie thought Deer-in-water looked *resplendent* (a word she'd lately learned) when he came to the center of the circular stage with a foot-tall headdress of porcupine quills and red horse-hair running down his back, a pink snapping-turtle-shell gorget the size of a turkey platter over his fur-trimmed gingham tunic, and white doeskin leggings fringed in gray goose feathers. In the center of the stage, a five-foot salting pan filled with firewood sat in an iron tripod, and before it was the microphone where Deer-in-water stood. Essie sat in a folding chair to one side of the stage, with her mother and the reporter and Deer-in-water's wife, away from the collapsible stands erected for the audience. She did not want to be mad at her mother any more, but she was. She wished she didn't yearn so badly to sing her father's song, but she did. So Essie sat.

Among the young men who danced in these competitions, the fashion that year was savage and minimal: high, furred moccasins and furred arm greaves dyed black or ox-blood red, dark loin-cloths tightly tucked, bone chokers, and headdress of a single, white, trailing feather that cut shapes in the air when the drums whirled the dancers to a finish. It was easy to admire their athletic art—each dancer performing his own extravagance on a traditional theme—but this season Essie took a fresh delight in watching lean, muscular, half-naked young men crouch and stomp and leap, one that made her blush and want to watch them longer, especially Howard Walkingstick. The scowls and grimaces that Howard used in his dance were so at odds with the quiet, genial boy he was that Essie almost laughed the first time she saw him rehearse. Tonight, however, she was all thirsty eyes as Howard spun around the fire that blazed in the salt pan, leaping like a ninja, prowling in a feral half-crouch, making a sudden double stomp to a tall stand-still with a final beat of the drum.

Deer-in-water gave each dancer a sip of the sweet water from a dipper-gourd and a taste of salt dried from the spring water that Essie had fetched that morning.

After the competitive dancing, the singers came on to open with their hymns. Essie went to the back of the stage where the performers entered. She held the flute to her chest when she sang "Amazing Grace" in Cherokee, accompanied by an electronic piano.

During the break that followed, Essie tried to avoid her mother in the crowd. She wandered among the ceremonial dancers putting on their brilliantly colored costumes: leathers and feathers and fabrics and beads in purple and blue and green and red, golden yellow, hot pink; headdresses insured for as much as a car. Among the social Stomp Dancers, the men wore tooled boots, blue jeans, pearl-buttoned western shirts, and cowboy hats with a single feather in the band; the women wore turtle-shell rattles on their legs beneath long Tear Dresses, with their rows of silver droplets at the throat, bust, hips and hem.

The second round of singing—traditional songs—introduced the ceremonial dancers who, because they were the stars of the fall pow-wow, had more than three-quarters of an hour all their own. So, once Essie had played the simple chant on her new flute and sung it in thanks to Green Corn Woman for bringing maize to the *Tsalagi*, she got a hotdog and a Coke and went back to the Visitors Center to change into jeans and sneakers and a nubby cotton sweater. She pulled her hair into a ponytail, got her mother's lip gloss from the office desk, and looked at herself in the mirror above the file credenza.

Everyone said she had his smile, but she felt something more of him in her. She could feel it when she sang his song. Even when she played it on the new flute, there was a swelling inside that wanted to burst from her chest, sing from her . . . soul, she guessed. There was something wonderful in that song, as though it sang her.

Returning to the pavilion, Essie met the reporter she'd hoped to avoid.

"Essie," she said, "hey. You never did tell me what you're doing for your"—she looked at her notebook—"your modern song."

"Oh," Essie said, "it's something you'll know."

The reporter smiled. "Okay, then. I'll be surprised. You go break a leg."

"*Wado,*" Essie said.

She would not sing the song.

When Essie reached the pavilion, the ceremonial dancers were finishing the Friendship Dance, having invited the audience to join them and link hands in a chain that the dance leader pulled serpentine around the fire, faster and faster to the drum, like a game of crack-the-whip, until everyone was laughing and staggering to keep a grip.

As the dancers left the stage, Harold Walkingstick came up to her and said, "How do you like the flute?"

Essie said. "It's your best ever, Harold. Really." Essie held the flute to her with both hands.

Harold grunted and said, "Yeah. Looks like you're in love."

"You wish."

Harold smiled. "You sound good tonight, Essie. I think you're set to win it all. But what are you gonna do for your modern? I mean, I know what you're *not* gonna do, huh?"

"Huh," Essie said. "I guess so."

Nearby, Deer-in-water said, "Singers, over here, please."

"See you, Harold."

"See you, Essie. Howard and I are rooting for you."

Deer-in-water had the singers draw numbered scraps of paper from a hollow gourd, and Essie drew number four. She tapped her toe idly while the first three girls all sang songs with "Oklahoma" in their titles.

"Our fourth performer this evening," Deer-in-water said into the microphone, "Essie Calico, doing . . . well, folks, she won't tell me."

The audience was still tittering as Essie came across the stage with the flute wrapped to her chest. Deer-in-water gave her a quizzical look, but Essie only smiled, avoided his headdress quills as she passed, and stepped behind the microphone.

She unfurled her arms and put the flute to her lips. There was a murmur from the crowd that quickly died as Essie played a trill that led to the opening notes of her father's song. By the time she reached the first chorus, Essie was alive with the music, tears—of joy, of relief—pooling behind her eyes, and at the second chorus, half the audience took it up.

Patches of beauty sign your name . . . .

Lost as she was in this moment, in the words the people sang, Essie could not keep a part of her from black imaginings of her mother storming the stage, destroying everything. She hadn't really meant to do this—had she? Salt tears and sweet music flowed from her.

Essie let the audience sing the last chorus acappella. Then she bowed and, on impulse, said into the microphone. "Tonight, *you* are my song. *Wado.*"

The crowd whooped its approval (Essie warmed to hear Howard Walkingstick's distinctive two-fingered whistle) as she retreated to the shadows at the back of the stage, turning a wet, happy face to Deer-in-water. As he, unruffled, introduced the next singer, Essie saw the reporter wave to her from beyond a clutch of Stomp Dancers and cup her hand to her mouth to shout. "Wow" was the only word Essie could make out.

Suddenly, she didn't know where she should go. Not to face her mother. Not back to the Center or out in the crowd. The reporter caught Essie in her indecision.

"Well," she said, "I guess you put a new twist on the singing convention, didn't you? Think the judges will go for it?"

"I . . . ."

"But, hey, you said I'd know the song. I kinda remember the

chorus. It used to be on the radio, didn't it?"

"Essie."

She turned to face her mother. Addy was in tears, but her face was not clenched in anger. It was sad, half-smiling. She opened her arms, and Essie, at once confused and relieved, stepped into their embrace.

Addy said, "I'm sorry. You didn't know, baby. I just realized. You didn't know."

"Didn't know?" Essie said.

Addy stepped back to look her daughter in the eye. "The song, baby. He wrote that for me, Essie. When I told him I was pregnant with you."

"This is fabulous," the reporter said, scribbling. "What is it? What's the name of the song?"

"'Calico Kites'," said Essie Calico, rising new to a difficult world that made other sense for her now, sense both salt and sweet.

Southern Gothic

My mother and her twin sister are both mad. Aunt Beth has her dead veteran's insurance and rides the bus all year long on a Golden Eagle pass. She wears a Roosevelt-era NRA eagle on her long gray coat. Thin socks topple over her tennis shoes. She sleeps between buses, surrounded by grocery sacks filled with cheap romances, sour socks, saltines, and mayonnaise, soaring on her madness off the slatted oak benches away from the red bugs and ticks along the Yazoo where she and my mother were born.

I am an only daughter and they say my mother used to look like me. I am always afraid that I or, worse, my daughter Blake will go mad. Does that sort of thing skip a generation or does it link them all? I think if my mother could die before I come unstuck that it would break the chain. It will never seem fair for Daddy to have died before her. There is tyranny in the chains of madness, but the democracy of death mocks justice too. I am glad Blake was not here. This summer she is with her father somewhere in Canada. She has never seen how my mother is. Never, never. I don't really know why I went to see my mother again. I still loved Daddy, that gentle and distant, gracious, complying man. And now he is dead. Died sometime while I was winding across the even flint spines of the ridges on the old highway on my way there.

Sunday, after church, he ate a plate lunch at the De Soto Cafe and walked home and died by the glider on the front porch. Aunt Beth, who never announces when she will visit herself upon the family, had

75

arrived from the bus station while he was out. That was why it was Beth Daddy saw leaning out of the door in what must have been his last light and thought she was my mother. In the warm and wisteria-shadowed summer light, incredulous and dazzled by pain, he must have mistaken her. He said, "It's all yours now, Diane. Take everything." He must have meant my mother. My name is Diane, but I don't look anything like my mother. Nothing. He must have been thinking of her. Aunt Beth thought it was a mistake too. She thought he was speaking to her.

He called me, a rare event, a week before he died, on the day Blake left with her father. I was stripping wax off the kitchen floor of my buckling old farm house where I live with Blake and her clean cats. Daddy could never understand why I live here. It's not that hard to keep clean, I told him. He brought my mother here once, three years ago, the last time he took her home. She sat in the car and cried the whole time, except when she saw Blake and frightened her, calling, "Diane. Diane, honey, come here." Blake says she doesn't remember. Daddy saw my high, white studio in the loft of the barn where my self portrait, my unfinished life's work, is hung, and then they left. My mother was very pale.

On the phone he seemed more eager to talk than I had ever known him to be, almost urgent. He asked questions: Was I glad I didn't have to teach this summer? (I was.) Did Blake still look like me? (She did.) Was I painting anything? (I was not, but I lied.) Near the end, he had not mentioned my mother, so I asked.

"She's fine, Dee," he said, then sighed. "She's fine."

"What does she do all day, Daddy?" I said, and I didn't have to. I had made my manners.

"She's content, Dee. She hardly even leaves her room. Oh, she's collected a lot of odds and ends in there and the place looks a little tacky, but at least she can live at home now. The new medications really work. She'll never have to go back, go away again. I can care for her now, Dee. I can."

I doubted it. Some nudge of guilt against my conscience urged me to see them. I struggled against it in a silence broken only by Daddy's taut breath crackling over the wires through time. I had not seen him in three years. I had not seen that house or my mother living in it since I was seventeen.

"She's talked about you, Dee," he said, startling the silence.

His urgency sent a wave of gooseflesh curling the down on my arms. The chill and guilt spread around me, over the polished wood and the plants. The loneliness in his voice transfused itself into my morning terror, my current creative "block," the big, empty house.

"Daddy," I said, "why don't I come down next weekend? I can take a few days."

He protested feebly, agreed, and then we hung up.

My mother has done crazy things all of my life and most of hers. She was up from Mississippi, in her first pair of ladies' leather shoes, visiting a maiden aunt when she met Daddy. She was very naïve then, and that good life he seemed to promise looked all roses. He wore a tie and hat every day, a thing that my mother had only known some bankers and the mortician in De Soto to do. He was a time keeper at the lumber mill, and he fell in love with her. They married. My mother softened her lye-soap chapped hands with Oil of Olay. Her expectations boggled reality and were never moved by it once. That first year she was happy with her expectations, with Daddy, and with me. She never went back to Mississippi.

The year after I was born the mill closed, and Daddy lost his job. My mother, bitten by shame and disappointment, insisted they could not let anyone know. Daddy had to leave for "work" each morning and come in at supper time to a maniacally scrubbed house. My mother always kept busy. I don't know what Daddy did all day. He never smoked. I know he did without lunch. On Fridays when the welfare commodities were issued, Daddy would put ours in two large, cardboard suitcases and tell my mother he had bought them black market. My mother loved the welfare food, saying that the government always keeps the best and gives it away to poor people and won't let decent folks buy a bite, anyway. After months of this, with half the town unemployed, Daddy pleaded with her one rainy day: "Darling, I don't *have* a job." My mother looked up from the dishes and smiled and said, "Of course you do, John." And he must have known it was done.

The next year Daddy got his job back. My mother got worse in other ways. She started writing a letter to Aunt Beth. My earliest memories are of her darting in and out of their bedroom several time a day to jot a line. The letter went on for weeks. One day she turned on the oven and, leaving it open, went in to write. After a few minutes she bolted from the house and ran to Daddy's office at the mill. She burst in and fell sobbing by his desk. He was out. A clerk came in and found her there. She stood up swelling with hysteria and asked the man fiercely whether there was a comma after "sincerely" in a letter and ran out. The clerk told Daddy, and he drove home looking for my mother and found me drowning in the gas on the kitchen floor.

When I was nine, my mother set fire to the curtains, and Daddy had to send her away for the first time. He later told me she did it because the Baptist minister had told her her problems were visited on her by God for something wicked she had done. Daddy became a Methodist after that, but he never made me go.

It was dark in the west the morning I left. A fork of summer lightning scribbled out of the clouds.

Aunt Beth or some neighbor, it was never clear which, had called the police. Daddy had already been taken away when I parked behind the sheriff's car. A town police car was in the front yard with its blue lights throbbing. Two men were in it. The sheriff and a deputy creaked in Daddy's glider. Jesus Christ, I was thinking, what has she done now? There's no ambulance. There's a white slice of moon in the sky. I walked toward the porch past the big chinaberry tree where two jays fought.

I recognized the sheriff as an old classmate of mine. He stood up and held my elbow gently while he told me what had happened. He was sorry. They were all concerned about my mother. They'd been waiting for the judge, if he could be found, to tell them what they could legally do for her. Now I was here, he'd go home. I asked if he could wait for a while in the car, and he said yes.

I stood at the door wondering whether I should knock or just walk in when Aunt Beth's round, cheesy face slid in behind the diamond-shaped pane. He lank gray hair was twisted up in rolling papers. She snatched open the door and a hot smell like rot and wet dogs poured out.

"Aunt Beth," I said, holding out my hand, less for comfort than to keep her away. "Aunt Beth, how is my mother?"

Her hands rolled around mine like cold dough. She was wearing her long coat. "Oh, dearie. Oh, Diane. I'm so glad, so glad. Your mama's fine, dearie. She doesn't know yet, of course. But everything's fine. I'm taking care of everything. You know it's all mine now."

I thought then that Aunt Beth was truly mad. "Aunt Beth," I said, "are you sure? Can you take care of my mother just for a little while?" I blinked back sweat in the heat.

"She won't get cold, Diane, dear. I have the furnace lit. I can stay here from now on. You know it's all mine now." She rolled her moon face to one side.

"Diane?" I heard my mother's voice. "I have a daughter named Diane."

She came up behind Aunt Beth and stood framed with her in the doorway. Her hair was matted like plugs of peat. Her hands, stunted little animals, pawed the hot breath of the house. "Do you know Diane?" she said. "I'm writing her a letter."

"Aunt Beth, please don't leave, " I told her. Don't go anywhere until I come back."

"We'll be fine, dearie," Aunt Beth said as I backed off the porch.

The sheriff helped me find the judge, who contacted a doctor and the funeral home for me. The doctor made arrangements with the state hospital to admit my mother the next day. I signed some papers for him. I signed more papers for the funeral director and sent a note to the Methodist minister. I checked into a motel and showered until I was very tired. When I went to sleep I dreamed I was Daddy, yet I was not, because I could look at him from outside. And still I knew his terrible longing for joy, any joy.

Aunt Beth led my mother out easily to the ambulance. I told my mother, yes, we are going to see Diane. Her vacant eyes smiled. "Diane?" she said. "Oh, yes. Look. It's all so clean."

I left her fondling the chrome valves and white sheets in the ambulance and walked into the house for the first time.

Aunt Beth was inside, on her hands and knees in the kitchen. She smiled up at me as I walked by the arch. I turned on the attic fan in the hall and pushed open the door to Daddy's room. It opened with a sucking *plop*. It was sealed all around with black rubber. Aunt Beth had stacked her goods in two pillowcases on his cot. She had not emptied the porcelain slop jar underneath it. There were papers on his desk: insurance, taxes, overdue bills. A crusted ring on the top of his bureau smelled of cologne. An old review of my first show was wedged in the mirror frame. In it, a Chicago critic said I had crystallized the hottest winds of the psyche as Leonardo had seen the liquid flame of motion and frozen it. It was not a good review. I took it. I didn't care about the watches, rings, and cologne Aunt Beth had collected in one pillowcase, but I wanted the other with Daddy's books on Dianetics and religion as a natural science. Outside one window was a bare patch of earth and a stepladder leaning against the house.

I shut Daddy's door and took Aunt Beth's pillage back to the living room. She came in from the kitchen when I called.

"Aunt Beth," I said, "you're going to have to go."

"But why, dearie?"

"Aunt Beth, there won't be anyone here. We're all going away.

She smiled at me and rolled her head.

"I want you to have what's in this pillowslip. Do you need any money, Aunt Beth?"

"No. Diane, can I make you some lunch, dear?"

"No, Aunt Beth," I said, trying to be gentle. "No, thank you. There is a bus going to Memphis this evening, if you want to take it." I smiled, picked up my purse, and left.

I returned the next day after the funeral. The furnace was off, but the fetid smell was even sharper. Aunt Beth was gone. She left a note for me on the door:

> Dear Diane,
> There was so much mayonnaise left
> over I did the kitchen floor with
> it for you.
> Love,
> Your Aunty Beth

I locked the house and hired a janitorial service to clean it.

Today they called while I was waxing the bannister. I told them I wanted to know what was in my mother's room. They found a piss-sodden mattress, moldy things in plastic bags. Her dresser drawers were all filled with tiny bits of paper. Each bit had a doodle or a name on it: John, Blake, Diane, Beth, and some others. There were paper chains strung in the closet with a name on every link.

I squeezed the golden wax in my hand. I held it in the sunlight, sleek, sparkling between my knuckles, It was like nothing I have ever seen. How significant, coherent, and understandable things are now. When Blake comes back, we will break the chain. I will have finished my portrait by then. She will love me for it. After we clean house, I will show her the old queen coiled fetal, feeding from the bloody bowl of her belly.

Gotham Gothic

Blake, Blake and her clean, sweet cats. Or the vagrant pains in her belly that give her a headache. Or will I bury her in New York if she dies here? That's all she can think about. Can we call the cats, and where will they take her when she gets sick, and what if she dies in the museum and never sees Pillow and Bandit again? Will they miss her? Will they know she's dead? Why can't she have a room by herself? I ask myself the same things.

Boodie says to me, "Lawz, Miss Dee,. It's nothing. She just stuck between two kinds of scared. Don't know if she wants to grow up or stay your little girl. Now, let's all go on up to that Met Museum, like you say. You just do your work; I'll see to our girl."

They say Boodie is a practical nurse. She is sweet and clean. That's why I hired her. That and because Blake says she has soft hands. They are. Her palms are the color of smoked cheese, lined and cross-hatched and soft as old chamois. She wipes tears from my cheeks with a corner of the sheet and pours me a glass of water to wash down my blue pill. Everything is alive this morning with a liquid, inner light.

I hear Blake turn off the shower. I gather my makeup and put on a thick hotel robe that smells of industrial soap. Boodie is dressed in gray slacks and a cardigan. She has on blunt shoes. I don't know when she got up. I like her face. It's not as old as her hands. It is radiant, mobile.

Blake comes out of the bathroom with a towel wrapped under her arms and another in a turban on her head. She turns sideways to go past me, her face to the wall. The hairs on her shoulders and neck are small and pale, each one of them distinct.

I say over my shoulder. "I'll have the granola and yogurt."

Blake says she wants the pizza, and I close the door of the bathroom behind me.

There are towels on the floor and one tucked neatly in a ring on the wall. There are only hand towels and wash cloths in the blindingbright steel rack above the toilet. I pick up the towels from the floor and drape them over the bars. The steam on the mirrors and the glass door of the shower is luminescent. I hang up my robe and pull on a flimsy shower cap. I can't feel any gray in my hair.

I am still dressing when room service knocks, and as I stuff my arms back into the damp robe, Blake throws open the door. I wrap the robe shut and hold it in place with my arm while I look for my purse. I don't know how much to tip in New York any more. I give the waiter five dollars. He smiles. I smile. I can't remember any Spanish. I think my robe must be gaping. I can smell its soap.

"You didn't say I couldn't have pizza," Blake says. She rolls up a slice, bites into it, and chews with her mouth open.

I button my blouse and unfold a sweater. It gets worse every time Blake comes home from her father's. She would rather be there than here, she says. Here is wherever I am. We are. Now us and Boodie. Boodie thinks she looks after us both. That's what they must have told her. Doctors will say things like that. The room-service cart glints beneath a starched white cloth. Blake is wearing blue jeans with ripped knees and a hooded sweatshirt and boots with soles thicker than Boodie's.

Boodie is saying to Blake, "We goin' to slip off while your Mama's at her work. I hear they got statutes there that she wouldn't want you to see." She chuckles and leans close to Blake. "You ever seen a naked man statute?" she says.

"Stop it," Blake says. "You are both so gross."

I am going to the Met to make sketches. Especially of the Riveras. I think the solidity will be good for me. I want the humming I

84

hear to change. To stop. I like the sheen of the yogurt and the way the granola catches the light. Later we will go down to SoHo, to the gallery where they're hanging my show. Hanging is what they call it here, even though it's mostly sculptures. Frieda is my agent. She knows about things like that. In Memphis they'd just say I'm showing my work.

The sky is molten with dark-bottomed clouds. The wind blusters. Blake walks ahead of us, hooded, her hands crossed over her belly in the kangaroo pouch of her sweatshirt. She slouches. She doesn't look at the sky. Boodie looks at everything. She holds my arm. We cross the parkway. Except for the man in a brown coat standing in an empty doorway saying, "Take a card, any card," the people on the sidewalks all have somewhere to go. Blake is one of them. I loop the strap of my purse over my head and pull it tight across my chest. Boodie does the same. Blake walks past the subway stop, and I have to call her back.

"Can't I just go to the movie or something?" she says. "I go to movies by myself at Dad's all the time."

Blake's father is Canadian. They do that in Canada. In Toronto. I tell her we don't do that in New York. In Memphis. She looks sidelong at the faces in the crowd coming up the steps from the subway.

Beneath the street, I buy tokens and give some to Boodie and Blake. I'm trying to make amends for the hard sounds of the station, the steel screams of the trains and the tiled echoes, black and white. We pass through the turnstile and wait. Blake stands with her back against a pillar, looking at her green boots, her face shrouded by the hood of her sweatshirt. I watch her. I look at the subway map on the wall.

Boodie says, "Nothin' like this in Memphis, is they, Miss Dee?"

"Not even Mud Island," I say. "You'll like the museum, Boodie. We'll eat at the restaurant there."

85

She says, "They got pizza?" And I laugh with her.

The train is not crowded. Boodie and I sit by the door. Blake stands, hanging from a strap, turning. She is graceful as an orangutan. We pass three stops. I look at the subway map. I tell Boodie we are on the wrong train. On the wrong side of the park.

"Then where they takin' us?" she says.

"To a Hundred and Twenty-fifth Street," I say.

"What's up there?"

I tell Boodie that it's in Harlem, but we can get a train back from there.

"Harlem?" she says. "I never seen Harlem, Miss Dee. Heard all about it, though. One of my uncles, he moved to Harlem. Said it's the black capital of America. All full of those Hate-ians and Rastos and whatnot."

"Blake," I say, "do you want to see Harlem? Boodie's never seen Harlem."

Blake shrugs and twirls on her strap. "Whatever," she says.

Boodie says, "We're on the A-Train, Baby. You know. Just like in that song."

The rhythm of these rails is sprung, syncopated with beats that shouldn't be. We surge north. Our minds go south. I think Boodie calls the clinic every night to tell them how I'm doing. Blake's father called me once while I was there. Blake wouldn't talk. I am so much better now that nothing is as clear as it was then. When I understood everything, it was too much to bear. That's why I had to sing. That's why they let me. Now I can watch my hands as they work. They do what they're told now.

The crowd on the platform at a Hundred and Twenty-fifth pours through the doors of the car, washing us back inside. Boodie holds my arm. Blake holds my other arm. Boodie says in her practical voice, "Come on now." She tugs on my arm. People bump us as we go against the flow. Blake flaps her hands around her hooded face. She screams, "Don't touch me. Let me out of here." And people do. They look at us and move aside.

I ask one of the policemen on the platform how to get back to the Met. I know that we are on the wrong side of the park, but he tells me that too. He talks about the D-train and the Number Five and going to the Bronx. I watch Boodie watching Blake.

"Lady," he says, "why don't you just go to the other platform and take the B back to Seventy-second and get a cab?"

I say, "Thank you." I mean it. The people in this crowd aren't going to the Met. They're waiting for another train. It stops. It has graffiti that breathes, but no one gets on. People get off, but they don't go anywhere. Three boys in red bandanas follow Boodie. The policeman walks toward them. I follow him. I take Boodie and Blake up on the street.

The sky is fluffed a dove pastel, dark now only in the dimples of the clouds. We walk with our backs to the wind.

"Let's get off this big street," Boodie says. "There's too much busyness goin' on here."

She's right. Faces move too fast here for my hands to fix their memory, except for the ones inside the shops and markets, the white and the Asian, and the man who grins through a window at me from a barber's chair. His face is bright and immobile, an ebony mask. The sheet that covers the rest of him is white. His face is not part of it.

We turn up a side street, and all the busyness falls away. There are children playing kickball. There are people standing on their stoops, sitting in folding chairs outside a grocery, waving to friends. I think that I could live here.

I say, "So, what do you think of Harlem, Boodie?"

"Why did you bring me here?" says Blake. She is walking between us. She has her hands folded across her chest. "I'm cold," she says.

"You'll warm up, Honey," Boodie says. "We'll just take us a fast stroll, make us a couple of left turns, and get right back on that train."

"Boodie wants to see Harlem," I say.

We turn left at a church, and in the alley behind it we see the jugglers' fair.

It's the fire eater I see first. He has flying dreadlocks and no shirt. There are scars on his chest. He belches a blue gout of flame. He leers at us and winks and takes a swig from a steel bottle and holds his torch in front of his face and roars another blast. There is a man with a box full of brown puppies. He juggles three of them. A hungry-looking boy squats over a scrap of blanket, his hands a blur as they shuffle three-card monte. The sides of the alley are lined with performers and flimsy booths made of cardboard and plastic pipe and sheets, where you can get your fortune told or buy juju beads by the cup. A cocoa-colored woman in a sequined cloche crooks her long finger at us.

"And right next to the church, too," Boodie says.

Blake says, "Let's go see. Can we?"

I don't have any change. I have subway tokens. I drop two in the fire eater's can. The people look right at us. We are the only ones not dealing tarot or break dancing or playing the pocket cornet. They smile. "Ladies," they say. "Ladies." They are eager, patient. Blake walks ahead of us. She looks at everything.

At the end of the alley there is a chain-link fence, and against it is a booth made from a piano crate, daubed with finger-painted symbols I have not seen before. They look familiar.

"You cold?" Boodie says to me.

There is no one else here at the end of the alley. The man in the booth smiles at us. He has hair the color of rusty water, a gold tooth, and green eyes, like Bandit, Blake's cat. He wears a topcoat buttoned to his throat. The cloth over the makeshift table in front of the booth is covered with figures like those on the outside. The man closes the book lying on it. It is a long, narrow book, with a maroon spine and time-ripened black covers that curl away from the pages. A ledger.

"Ladies," he says. "You have come to the right place." I do not recognize his accent.

Blake tosses the hood off her head. Her hands burrow in the pocket pouch. "What do you do?" she says.

I look at the drawings on the crate, on the cloth. I must have seen them somewhere before. Runes or something African. It is on the tip of my memory.

"Five minutes of madness," the man says. "That's all."

I look at him. A smile darts across his lips. I start to speak.

"No questions," the man says. "Do you want it or not?"

"Miss Dee," Boodie says, "let's go on out of here. We not supposed to be here."

"Only the finest madness," the man says.

"How much?" Blake says.

The man waves a long, skinny finger at her. "No questions, little sister," he says. He keeps his eyes on mine. They are like jade, like fissured fire.

"We didn't come here looking for drugs," I tell him.

"Miss Dee," Boodie says, "come on now. You'll get your head busted and all your money stole."

The man shows the palms of his hands, a gesture of surrender. His palms are blushed with henna that has caked in the creases like dried blood. They look soft, like Boodie's. I want to touch them, pick in their creases with my nail. I want to steal the color from his eyes. I want to paint with his hands.

"And we're not looking for love," I say. "What else do you have?"

"Mom," Blake says. "Come on."

The man closes his eyes and opens them slowly. He lowers his chin and shakes his head. "Think on it," he says. "I'm always here. I'll be here when you come back."

The crowd has grown. Blake and Boodie pull me into it. I look back, but there are too many people; I can not see the booth at the end of the alley. My ears are full. I can not hear the flutes or congas or the song of the woman with the accordion.

The wind hits us in the street. Boodie pulls me to the left. My ears pop and clear.

"You cold?" Boodie says.

I say, "I want some coffee."

We turn left again and find a diner and go inside and sit at the counter. I order coffee for us, hot chocolate and a sticky bun for Blake.

"What do you think he meant?" I say.

"Meant?" says Boodie. "Why, I imagine! Fine minutes of madness—whatch you think he meant? Get you robbed and raped, that will."

I say, "Five minutes, Boodie. He said, 'Five minutes of madness.' Didn't he, Blake?"

She picks at her sticky bun and sings softly, *"Five is fine, and fine is five. How do you know that you're alive?"*

She wags her head in tempo, stirring cocoa with her finger. I hear myself in her voice. She doesn't know her danger, what that sound can do. I know. I used to sing too.

Boodie holds her cup in both hands. "I'm just glad to be alive," she says. "You see that man's hands? What's a man that'd do his hands up like that for? What's he up to?"

"I want to know," I say. "Was it 'five' or 'fine'?"

"Whichever," Boodie says. "You let somebody else come along and take that kind of fineness, Miss Dee."

"What," I say, "and give it away to a stranger? That was ours, Boodie."

"What was," she says. She turns on her stool to look at me.

"That's right," I say. "What was it? Boodie, we can't come all the way to Harlem and go home without knowing, can we?"

"It's too cold," Blake says.

Boodie says, "Sit down, Miss Dee. Please."

I put money on the counter. "Wait here," I say. "Fifteen, twenty minutes. Just wait. I'm coming right back."

Boodie says something as the wind blows the door shut behind me.

I turn right and right again. The morning repeats itself in the clouds. Places always look strange when you come to them from a different way. I turn and look behind me. Have I seen these moving faces before? I walk two steps backward, stumble, turn again. There is no church on this street. Have I walked one block or two? I breathe. I retrace my steps back to where I've been. I sing, *"Goin' back to where I been."* Two girls in quilted jackets stick out their butts and snap their fingers. "You go on down there," one of them says. I do. The buildings bulge toward the sidewalk. Yes, I remember the dry cleaners and the shoe shop and the building with its steel curtain shut. A block's a long way in New York. I go right at the second one. The wind tosses my hair around my face. I peel away the strands that catch in the corners of my mouth. Day hums in my ears.

The mouth of the alley is gagged by a crowd watching two acrobats. They run up the wall of the church and flip backward. They do shoulder kips. The crowd whistles and claps. I hold my purse against me with both hands and shoulder my way around the back of them. I hurry past the monte dealer and the puppy juggler and the woman in the sequined cloche who is smoking a cigar. She is an astrologer, her sign says. I feel like I have just understood something for the first time, something I've always known. I know I've felt this way before. I believe the man with green eyes knows it too. He knows all he can give me is what's mine.

I come out of the crowd at the end of the alley. I check my purse and my hair. I walk toward the piano-crate booth. There is a sheet hung over it. On the sheet is a message drawn in black fingerpaint: Back In Fine Minutes. I look back at the crowd. I go to a man selling watches from a box slung around his neck.

"Where is he?" I say. "The man in that booth?"

"Mister Fine?" he says. "He always put that up. You like a nice watch? Something for everyday?"

"Will he be back?" I say.

"Oh, he always be back," the watch man says. "If not today, tomorrow. This one here's a real Rolodex."

I left it here and he took it with him. He took my fineness with him. I walk flatfooted. I weave. I glance off shoulders and backs. Dark faces scowl. They ask me am I drunk. A woman pushes me. I stumble. It was almost all so clear, understandable, coherent, the way I know things used to be, the way they say it's not anymore. And he has it. Or someone else does. Someone else came. She took mine with her, and I don't know where she's gone. A big man in a Tyrolean hat helps me out to the street.

A police car stops, and Boodie gets out of it. Blake is in the backseat, her head hooded and bowed like a criminal's.

Boodie holds my shoulders. I cry. I say, "Don't let her know. Don't let her know it can be like this. I almost found out, Boodie. If I just knew how, I could tell her. Save her."

The policeman comes up. "Everything okay here?" he says. "Is this who you're looking for?"

"It's okay," Boodie says. "Everything's all right. She just skimmin' the top off some old misery, that's all. Give her five minutes. She goin' to be fine."

Le Ba Dien's War

. . . and there are no indications of hostile activity in the Khe Nan Valley. Base potential: nil.

From the Termination Report of Captain Edward Aldous, USMC, re: Operation *Partizan*, Khe Nan, RSVN. 3Sept66

Yes, he told the American captain, he knew that as headman he could be held responsible for the girls—and women, married women—selling themselves to the men on the perimeter at night, and for the boys who grew the dinky-dou weed, even for the ration cans pilfered from the dump. But what could he do? He could not be everywhere. If youth will disobey, it will disobey. Of course he was pleased the Americans had come, but he had not asked them. He could not be everywhere at once. And what else was there for the youth to do as . . . interesting as American marines? Or, to be frank, as profitable?

Captain Aldous was a practical man. "What," he said, "would keep them in, Mr. Dien? My men are out there to protect this village, and they can't do that high on dope or screwing some honeywa in their positions. We've got to put a stop to it."

"Will your men not obey either, sir?"

Aldous paced the headman's packed-earth courtyard from the ginkgo tree that shaded it to the dung heap by the melon patch.

"Dammit, man, it's your security I'm talking about."

Le Ba Dien swept the air with his hand and said, "Then why have you not circled the village, sir?"

"You're civilians, Mr. Dien. If it came to a fight, your village would be needlessly exposed."

"Not with you protecting us."

Aldous snapped a twig from the ginkgo tree, leaned against the trunk, and began stripping leaves. "It's bad tactics, Mr. Dien. I know you don't understand, but it's a matter of exposure. We don't like to, well . . . ."

"To put your backs to us, sir?"

The headman's grin was thoroughly inscrutable to Aldous. He threw down the twig. "Is it just a question of money, Mr. Dien?"

Le Ba Dien agreed that Khe Nan was a poor village.

Aldous sighed. He removed his helmet, mopped his face with a green handkerchief, and stood away from the tree. He seemed, to Le Ba Dien, relieved by the village's poverty. "Mr. Dien," he said, "I have been authorized to put money in circulation here, for that very reason, but only if we can find some honest exchange of labor—say, digging gun pits for the howitzers. How does that sound?"

This was the first Le Ba Dien had heard about howitzers. Was Khe Nan to be a fire base after all? Perhaps these marines did not intend to stay just three months and then leave, as the Green Berets had done last year, living with the loinclothed, barbarian Bru montagnards on the mountain ridge. The Green Berets and the Viet Cong who came to challenge them laid ambushes and land mines along the trails on the montagnard ridge, and Le Ba Dien had been wounded in the hip by one of them. Whether American or Viet Cong he did not know. That had been a bad time in Khe Nan Valley, and a permanent Marine base would be worse. Le Ba Dien was a patient man, long schooled in war and its costs.

He said, about hiring the youth to dig gun pits, "Yes. Yes, that might be very good—until harvest."

94

"Now, about getting those . . . people to stay off our perimeter at night," Aldous said, "I could get films dropped in, or—"

"—or television or hi fidelity." Le Ba Dien had to smile. "Look there, sir." He pointed toward the bare power poles that staggered down the mountain from the old plantation villa hidden in the jungle a kilometer above. There has been no electricity here since 1954," he said, "except for the CARE generator the Viet Cong took. Before that, the youth would listen at night to the jazz broadcast from Hué."

On board the helicopter that came in two days later were a Honda generator and an AM/FM/shortwave radio that could receive from as far away as Phnom Penh, where the Hindus broadcast monkey chants. Le Ba Dien showed the villagers that their radio had many more dials than the one the bandy-legged, stone-age Bru got from the Green Berets. And everyone except old Cao, the village charcoal maker who had fought against the French, agreed it was an excellent gift.

Two marine artillerymen who came in on the helicopter were dispatched to search for the surveyors' benchmark in the old plantation's overgrown banana groves. Le Be Dien sent six men with axes and knives to help them find it. One of the village men said he knew what they were looking for: a brass disc half the size of a winnowing pan set in a slab of concrete.

He led them high up the side of the trail-veined ridge, to just above the stuccoed French villa, then quartered back down the slope until they found it. The two artillerymen were breathing through their mouths. One of them rolled up his trouser leg and found a leech the size of a hair. The boys from Khe Nan covered their smiles as the leech curled under the marine's cigarette and he made faces and spat. Before leaving, the artillerymen told the boys to clear the ground around the benchmark and enough of the jungle from the hillside to let the village be seen.

The boys ate rice and *noucmam* cooked in their tin pails, and the marines went down the ridge toward the river, searching for a ford. When the Americans were out of sight, the boys dragged the marker to the next lowest bench on the ridge, where they began their clearing. At evening they overtook the two artillerymen, their maps out, still searching for a way across the cold river that plows its seasonal course through the Khe Nan Valley.

For three days the marine surveyors worked back and forth between the benchmark and the village, computing altitudes and siting positions for their guns.

Le Be Dien passed word of the American guns to the Bru through the woodcutters who sold Cao the billets he burned into charcoal. Cao disapproved of Dien's dealing with the Bru.

The next day, Le Ba Dien rode his bicycle to the Esso store at the foot of the cataracts where the semi-paved road crossed the river. He came back pushing his bicycle, three fighting cocks in coops and a jerrycan of gasoline for the generator roped to the frame. His hip ached from its wound, and he was short of breath when he saw the captain.

"You've been very helpful, Mr. Dien," Aldous said, "and I want you to know we appreciate it."

Le Ba Dien nodded.

"We'll be finished surveying by tomorrow, and the boys can start on those gun pits any time. The pay'll be a hundred piasters a day. Fair enough?" It was one dollar American.

Le Ba Dien leaned his bicycle outside his door. "Yes," he said. "It is generous."

"They will earn it."

As the captain trooped down the main path past the palms by the village pavilion, Cao slipped from behind Le Ba Dien's haycock and spat a gout of betel in the marine's dusty print. Cao's singed arms and face were gritty with black ash, and there was a pale band across his brow where a sweat rag had been tied. He smelled, like the village, of *noucmam* and wet ash. He sucked his slick lower lip against his gums, the lip and gums bright red from the betel he chewed.

"Yankee Zippo dogs. Yellow curs." Cao turned to the headman. "They'll burn us when they leave, Dien. Mark me."

Le Ba Dien shook his head and said, "Take some of my hay you came to steal, old man. Go bank your fires."

Cao chewed solemnly and stared toward the the fallow paddy where the Americans were bivouacked. Finally, he spat again and looked at the cocks in the coops that Le Ba Dien was stacking.

"There," he said, pointing to a Phu Bai red's purple ruff. "I've seen that color before, from a ridge above Dien Bien Phu as the sun came up. Is it cockfights then? With the montagnards?"

"Yes, old fighter. Will you go and tell them?"

The less Cao saw of the Americans the better. The longer they stayed, the less Cao hid his contempt for them. Old as he was, Cao was not beyond mischief that the Americans could see as hostile. And if there were trouble, it would be Le Ba Dien who answered for it.

"When shall we pit the birds, Dien?"

"It will take a week to put our birds in trim. Harvest will start in two, so at least by then."

"And the Americans? Will they come?"

"Yes."

Cao linked his blackened little finger in Le Ba Dien's, his finger the French Legionnaires burned the nail from, and said, "Let me tell you, headman, it is foolish to trust a round-eye."

Le Ba Dien returned the grip. "I trust them, old fighter, to do what they will do. So hurry and be back before night. The claymores will be armed after dark."

When Cao had not returned at dusk, Le Ba Dien was worried. He banked the old man's charcoal pits with wet hay and walked back to the pavilion where the new generator had been set up. He dragged a

97

stick along a garden fenced with woven branches. The ashes were uncomfortable beneath his shirt. The Viet Cong had not been back since they took the other generator. So why were the Americans here? There was nothing for them here. Still, they had come. And soon the Viet Cong would return if they did not leave. It was only a matter of time until they heard of the howitzers. Cao. Though the old man had moved the magazine portrait of Ho Chi Minh inside his door, he still talked too much. It seemed to Le Ba Dien that age would bring Cao neither temperance nor wisdom. The old man would always remember feeling most alive with the Vietminh, a Lebel carbine snapping against his shoulder. It had been Cao who rashly stole grenades from the Green Berets. Yes, Cao troubled him, but Le Ba Dien understood how he felt. And he knew what shrapnel does, how it sings in the high grass, clicking like scythes. The land mine on the ridge that gave him his wound had killed his wife.

A dozen children, the oldest no more than thirteen, with streaks of the paddies' black mud caking on their legs, were chattering in the tin-roofed pavilion when Le Ba Dsien came in. He turned on the generator with the key around his neck and jerked the motor to life. The single light bulb hung from the ceiling flickered to life and the radio spat static until he found the weak signal from Hué carrying a fast saxophone tune. He called to a tall boy with a cast to one eye and an impetigo sore above his ear. Le Ba Dien told him to keep the signal tuned in, then went to meet Captain Aldous and his red-faced gunnery sergeant walking into the village on the wide main dike.

The captain gave Le Ba Dien a bottle of American whiskey and said he was pleased that boys were already showing up to work on the gun pits. He slapped the gunnery sergeant on the shoulder and said, "Gunney, we need to congratulate the headman here on the excellent cooperation he's provided."

Le Ba Dien saw that the bottle was not full. The marines had obviously been drinking, and it seemed best to invite them into the pavilion, where one of the older girls brought them three glasses and a jar of water.

Le Ba Dien sat sweating with the marines in a corner away from the ring of children swaying to the music in front of the radio. He told the captain the whiskey was good.

"I'm glad you like it, Mr. Dien," Aldous said. He leaned forward in his plastic chair, resting his elbows on his knees. "Tell me," he said, "have the Viet Cong been back since the Special Forces team left?"

"The Green Berets?"

"Yes."

"No."

"Mr. Dien, I want us to have what I'd call candid relations with you people. I want us to be able to be honest with each other."

Le Ba Dien said he also hoped so.

"So," Aldous said, "is the jungle between here and the ridges mined?"

"Once," Le Ba Dien said, "a woman of our village was killed by a land mine on the montagnard ridge."

And the shrapnel whined in the high grass.

"Where?"

"Past Monkey Mountain, on the path near the shrine of worship."

The radio squealed harshly, and a woman's voice announced in English that Radio Hanoi had liberated the frequency. The woman began greeting American marines and their units by name. She said the marines in Khe Nan should enjoy their holiday, while it lasted.

Aldous stared at Le Ba Dien, searching his face for a reaction, wondering whether the headman had chosen that station by design.

The whiskey was stronger than rice wine, hot in Le Ba Dien's ears. He wondered whether the captain knew that the "woman of our village" had been his wife, and would that make the captain wary of him. He looked out at the gathering darkness beyond the ring of children.

Finally, music began, and the gunnery sergeant said, "Hell, Skipper, she pulls them names out of a hat."

Aldous and Le Ba Dien laughed.

Walking back to the bivouac along village paths where dinner fires and charcoal stoves glowed outside the doorways of thatch huts, Aldous drank from the glass of whiskey he still held. Dien was a strange little buzzard, he thought. He seemed eager to cooperate, and was definitely the political weight in the village, but Aldous still felt there were things the headman wasn't telling him, not being completely straight about. Aldous emptied his glass and shrugged. Oriental inscrutability, he supposed.

Le Ba Dien turned off the radio and sent the children home soon after the marines had gone. The headman was fatigued and woozy from the whiskey, his nerves brittle as rice straw. Before leaving, the captain had asked him where the village's young men were. Le Ba Dien said they were in the army. He was glad the captain had not asked whose. Le Ba Dien did not—indeed, cared not to—know. It was all one to him. He had intended to bring up the cock fights, but in his concern for Cao had forgotten. If the old man were rash enough to come in at night past the American perimeter, Le Ba Dien could only fear the worst.

The three cool, thatched rooms of his house seemed too large, and he could not sleep. He counted the copy books he would be teaching the children from after the harvest, ate half a melon and some rice and brought the three fighting cocks inside into the lantern light. With a pair of scissors, he clipped the birds' combs, plucked under-breast feathers from each of them. From the Phu Bai red he snipped wing feathers also. Then he imped these feathers back on with thin straw and rice paste. Le Ba Dien judged the red to be the best of the three, but with its wing feathers imped and folded under, it would be awkward. Still, the feathers had to be strong enough to hold up through a fight. He took out three sets of steel spurs and dulled them with a file.

Le Ba Dien put his wife's scissors back in their box. Perhaps Cao should come live with me, he thought. It was not good for the old man to live alone, and Le Ba Dien thought he might keep an eye on Cao that way, perhaps keep him alive. Later, Le Ba Dien blew out the lantern and lay in his hammock listening to the heat.

When at last he slept, he dreamed of her in a conical straw hat of newly woven yellow, the young woman at the fair, in loose white pants and ao-dai, who abhorred the cock fights he lived by that summer after his year at the University of Hué. She was a coast girl from a bustling town where ice was sold each day. Yet she had carried red tiles from the old villa on a shoulder pole, and together they built the roof now above him. Then the Vietcong and the Red River men in khaki came, and then the Green Berets. And then there were the ambushes and land mines on the trail they took to the shrine.

The explosion ripped him from sleep. He disengaged the ring of aftershock from the aching dream of his wife, blurted Cao's name, and dropped to the packed earth floor. Two bursts of automatic fire—a long and a short—followed, then the sounds of the Americans crying out orders on their perimeter. "Oh, Cao," he whispered. "Oh, fool."

He rushed from his house, past huts where women stood holding crying infants. A pair of young marines were nervously fanning their bayoneted rifles at the young boys gathered where the main dike's path spread into the village. An illumination flare was sputtering in the sky. The silhouettes of two girls hurrying from the perimeter darted behind the marines and disappeared into a melon arbor. One of the marines pointed his rifle at the boys and shouted at Le Ba Dien to send them home.

Le Ba Dien realized that it was over, Cao, no doubt, dead. All he could hear now were the frogs in the paddies, a pig snorting in a nearby sty. He told the boys to go home. But the cast-eyed boy with the impetigo scar above his ear held back, and Le Ba Dien remembered that he was Cao's niece's's son.

The boy fixed Le Ba Dien with his wandering eye and said, "It was my uncle, wasn't it, headman?"

Le Ba Dien took his hand and walked him toward the pavilion.

"No," Le Ba Dien said, himself unwilling to accept Cao's death. "But I should not have asked him to go up the ridge so late. He is too old."

A voice behind them bellowed, "When I am too old to find my way into my own village at night, put me in my deepest pit and fill it."

Le Ba Dien and the boy turned to see a cross, exceptionally-sooted Cao standing, arms akimbo, at the door of his hut.

"Go to bed, nephew," Cao told the boy, then turned to Le Ba Dien. "They will do what they will do, remember, Dien?"

The boy tripped over his feet as he left, staring at Le Ba Dien who was squatted on his heels giggling softly in relief.

Cao spat and said, "I saw your American friends when I came in, Dien. The animals were pissing in one of my pits. I tried, but there was no saving that charcoal. Do you know what it will smell like if it's burned?"

Le Ba Dien smiled at him. "Like montagnards, old man?"

"Yes," Cao said. He stuffed pounded betel in his cheek.

After dawn, the marines dragged the water buffalo that had wandered into their mines back to the village. It was stiff by then, flies swarming its muzzle. Later, the helicopters came, bringing only two guns. It was as well. The boys would not go to dig after the water buffalo was killed. The marines had to do their own sandbagging, and someone took two of their shovels.

Two days later, sitting in the pavilion with Le Ba Dien, Aldous stacked a pile of new piasters on the table beside the radio.

"Fifteen thousand," he said. "That's a lot for one wataboo, Mr. Dien."

Le Ba Dien said yes, that they are more difficult to get now.

"My men tell me that the girls have quit coming to the perimeter at night," Aldous said, "except for an old fat one who drinks."

"A montagnard, sir. They will mate with apes."

Aldous considered this reply. "Tell me," he said, "is there something wrong Mr. Dien?"

"That I cannot keep one drunken Bru rock-ape from raising her skirts?"

"Why won't the boys come help with the digging? Didn't you tell them to? And the women won't do our laundry anymore. Your people are beginning to act like they're afraid of us, Mr. Dien."

Le Ba Dien shook his head slowly. "You have sensed it too," he said.

"Mr. Dien," Aldous said, "is there anything we can do to, to make things right again?"

Le Ba Dien shot his eyebrows and raised a finger. "Do you remember the cocks I brought in last week? I think I may have just the plan." He reached to touch the captain's hand in that universal Vietnamese gesture of friendship.

Aldous drew his hand away. "Cocks?" he said.

"Fights," said Le Ba Dien. "Chicken fights. You should come. It would show your solidarity."

At his house, while the captain looked at the birds, Le Ba Dien saw a patrol leaving the perimeter. He asked the captain about this.

"The artillery observer wanted to take a look around."

"Hunting, sir?"

"Oh, yes."

Gunners swarmed over the howitzers the next morning. People

working in the nearest paddies saw the gunners cover their ears. Two lanyards were snapped, and the guns roared, buckling back in their carriages. Seconds later and four kilometers across the valley, a pair of silent white jets of smoke rose on the side of Monkey Mountain. The came the muffled *whumps*, like distant drums. An officer dashed from the artillery tent. He looked at the smoke through his binoculars, at the map in his hand, and called over his shoulder to the men standing at the charts inside the tent. The howitzers fired again, and again hit the mountain. People began cheering. An old woman beat an iron spoon on a rendering vat. Workers waved from the paddies.

Another officer came out to look through the guns' sights. A third salvo hit the same mark. Even the farthest dike menders began to hurrah.

Le Ba Dien saw the captain coming from the perimeter in long, quick strides, his face clouded, taped dog tags slapping his drenched undershirt. Le Ba Dien held his breath to keep from smiling: moving the benchmark had had its effect.

"Stop this. Shut these people up," the captain shouted.

"Sir?"

"What the hell is going on?"

"Sir," Le Ba Dien said, "I told them to show support for your efforts."

"Support? What the hell for?"

"Your excellent marksmanship, I suppose, sir." He gestured toward Monkey Mountain. "There were three hits the same."

"Our target," the captain said between his teeth, "was on the *other* side of the damn mountain."

"Viet Cong, sir?"

"Hell, yes," the captain said. Then, after a moment, added, "Bound to be."

"I am sorry. No one knew. Please tell your men."

The days before the harvest were tense but busy ones for Le Ba

Dien. There were paddies to drain, threshing and winnowing sheds to be readied. Women gathered each day to cut bindings and sharpen sickles. Marine patrols came and went daily now, but the big guns squatted silent in their pits. The montagnard woodcutters brought no news of Viet Cong.

A child came to Le Ba Dien and said that two montagnards wanted to see him at Cao's charcoal pits. The fronds of the unpruned banana grove surrounding the pits were tattered and black with soot, like a smudge on the jungle at the edge of the village farthest from the American bivouac. As he entered the grove, Le Ba Dien saw Cao measuring a stack of wood with a notched stick and paying the woodmen. Cao had not spoken to him since the night the water buffalo was killed. The montagnards squatted beneath a banana tree counting their piasters.

Cao narrowed his eyes and gestured with his sparsely whiskered chin. "They want to know when we'll be ready to fight our birds," he said and stepped down into one of his pits.

Le Ba Dien put his fingers to his lips and whistled. "Two days," he called, holding up his fingers.

The Bru rose, clicking in their dialect, and one waved two fingers as they left.

"Don't let the Zippo curs see you," Cao said. "They might think you love the Bru best."

"Someone is wanting to make the Americans feel unloved," said Le Ba Dien. "One of their claymore mines is missing."

"Why come to me? What would I want with a mine?" Cao put down his folding shovel and pointed to his chest. "In a week, I could have a Browning rifle. I could have a mortar."

"Peace, Uncle Ho," Le Ba Dien said, throwing up his hands. "I only told them I would ask. Please. I need you, old one, at the fights. Someone must keep a bank while I handle the birds."

"The Americans will bet too?

105

"So they say. And, yes, also the montagnards."

Cao chewed in silence. "Americans are rich—a very fat people," he said. "What do they care to lose their money? Will that make them leave us?"

"They will go when they have had enough."

"Enough of smiles and fawning and rooster fights?"

"Enough of us, old man. Enough of us."

Cao spat and picked up his shovel.

"Is that a new shovel?" Le Ba Dien said, pointing to the marine entrenching tool in Cao's hand.

Bru tribesmen in loincloths and strange earrings made of ivory and teak began to appear in Khe Nan early on the day of the fights, haggling with women over Michelin sandals and trading warped crossbows to the Americans for cigarettes. At late afternoon, Aldous came to the pavilion to see the montagnard birds and found Le Ba Dien helping to assemble the fighting pit. The captain said he would be bringing a dozen or so men. A goodwill gesture, he called it.

"There will be three odds-makers," Le Ba Dien said, "but bet with old Cao, sir, not the Bru. It would be an insult otherwise."

The captain, one of his lieutenants, an artillery officer, the red-faced gunnery sergeant, and several other marines came back an hour later. The Bru were huddled on one side of the makeshift log pit, clicking over their birds and smoking American menthol cigarettes. Cao and the two Bru odds-makers were filling their aprons with hollow rubber balls and betting slips cut from colored paper. Each ball had been slit to open like a coin purse when it was squeezed. The money and betting slips were placed inside and thrown back and forth between the bookies and the bettors. The balls began to arc across the pit as the Bru handler walked the perimeter holding up his first bird, and Le Ba Dien did the same with his red. Whistles and shouts drove up the odds, which could change with every wager. Marines waved and shouted in pidgin for the balls.

The man acting as the pit boss called out, "Pit them," and the birds were released a meter apart in the center of the pit.

The birds lowered their heads and circled. The montagnard bird was a ruff-necked yellow, lighter than the red, but with good legs and the small, flat head of a krait. The red carried the first charge by its weight and struck lung. A bubble of blood stood on the yellow's nare when they separated the birds. On the second pass, each bird tangled its spurs in the other's tail.

"Handle them."

The Bru handler sucked blood from his bird's lung through its beak, but its head had begun to weave and sink. The third time, the yellow could not clear the ground. It spread its ruff in defiance as the red leapt and scored behind each wing with its dull spurs. The yellow blinked and dropped its head in the sand.

The marines lost heavily when Le Ba Dien's second bird was outclassed by a lithe black, and the third's plucked breast failed to turn an otherwise glancing gaff. The finale would be the black against the Phu Bai red.

Aldous elbowed his way to the edge of the pit. "We're all for that red, Mr. Dien," he said. "The gunney there says he knows chickens, and that red looks like a good one to him. He can take that black bird, can't he?"

"Thank you for your support, sir."

Held beak to beak, the birds gouged at each other's eyes, their thin necks stretched taut as trip wires. The betting increased, with the odds-makers leaping in and out of the pit to retrieve collided balls. The marines peeled more piasters off their rolls.

Pitted, the birds circled, each pecking ineffectually at the other's clipped comb. The black sprang first, fell and landed on its back, a curved spur in each of the red's wings. They beak-fought until the call came to handle them. The betting had become a frenzy.

Le Ba Dien spat in his bird's face to cool it and felt for the weakly imped feathers, found one, and folded it, unnoticed, beneath the wing.

As the birds circled again, fanning the sand, the red's bent feather lodged between its wing and ribs. But even off balance, the red's weight was telling. Twice it might have won the match, but the spurs Le Ba Dien had dulled found only flesh and feathers, no organs. The birds bristled their necks and flurried heel to heel, but the black could never get as high as the red's unprotected breast. The red hissed, cawed, leapt above the black, but could not make an end. The balls continued to fly. The red leapt again, missed the agile black, and furrowed the sand with its beak. Its next leap carried it onto the log wall around the pit, and from there into the gunnery sergeant's face.

The sergeant batted the bird down and, shouting, "Sonofabitch," stomped blindly where it fell.

The artillery officer screamed, "Mother fucking loser," and brought a heel down on the flapping bird. The marines made a tight circle and kicked the bird to death. The black crowed in the middle of the pit. The marines stopped and realized what they had done. They went silent. The dead bird was covered with fallen betting slips.

As the marines milled about, and Cao calculated their losses, the gunnery sergeant lifted the red by its shattered wing. Feathers came off in his hand, and he recognized the straw imps in the wing. Aldous heard him mutter, "Slimy goddam gook." The sergeant unsheathed the K-Bar strapped to his boot and vaulted into the pit. Before the captain could stop him, he had Le Ba Dien in a choke-hold from behind, the flat of the knife against his kidney, saying, "All right, you slope-head sonofabitch, what the fuck you done?"

The crowd fell away, and Aldous broke through them "At ease, gunney," he said. "Let him go."

The gunnery sergeant released Le Ba Dien roughly and stepped back. "Skipper," he said, "that goddam bird was rigged. Swear to god, it was rigged."

"At ease. Now," Aldous said. "Put up your pig-sticker and get the men out of here. Mr. Dien, can we step outside for a minute?"

Resting one hand on the wall of the pit and rubbing his throat with the other, Le Ba Dien nodded.

They walked to Le Ba Dien's tile-roofed hut and stood beneath the ginkgo tree.

"Mr. Dien," the captain said, "I suppose the gunney was right about the bird."

Le Ba Dien said he was.

"You don't want us here, do you, Mr. Dien?"

Le Ba Dien said he had not asked them to come.

The captain rubbed his chin. "I don't know what you are, Mr. Dien," he said, "but you are no coward."

Within two days, the howitzers were gone. The marines were pulling out. The captain had given no word.

Le Ba Dien and Cao stood in the smoky charcoal grove, watching the last helicopter as it lumbered over the banana tops and out of sight.

"They must think you a great fool, Dien, to lose a fine bird like that red," Cao said.

"Cao," Le Ba Dien said, "do you think we might keep the new radio?"

"Why ask me. It was a gift from your friends."

"I saw you with the chief sergeant before the helicopters came. What was in the sacks you gave him?"

"Charcoal. I saved it for them to cook fresh beef over when they get back to Phu Bai."

"From the pit the night the water buffalo was killed?"

"The same."

"You are a wicked man."

109

Cao squatted beside a mound of earth thrown from a fresh pit and dug in it until he uncovered a canvas pack and a shoulder bag. He took a large tin can and a beer opener from the pack and began punching holes in the sides of the can, top and bottom.

Le Ba Dien fingered the stack of money in his own bag.

"Part of this money goes to the Bru," he said. "Do you want to take it to them, old friend?"

"Take it yourself," Cao said. He handed Le Ba Dien a wad of betting slips. "Money for your wife in heaven. Burn it for me at the shrine."

Cao then took a claymore mine from his pack and pried open the back, rolled a pinch of its plastic explosive into a cone, put it on the ground, and lit it with a stiff, new Zippo. He put the perforated can over it and placed his blackened cooking pot on top.

"What is for dinner, Cao?"

"Rice. And chicken."

"Please," said Le Ba Dien, "not my red."

Cao began taking tins of C-ration meat from his pack.

"For my excellent charcoal," he said.

White Bear

Unlike their friends the Mitchells, Tom and Maggie Harrison were fearless of the future. But there was no future the Harrisons could contemplate for Jane and Mike without sadness and disbelief. It was over for them. PTSD, the doctors said: post traumatic-stress disorder. Mike's fits of rage and blind frustration, his nightmares about being blown from the mouth of a cave, his weeks-long despondencies were all delayed reactions to his tour in Vietnam. It was happening to a lot of Vietvets, the doctors said, now that men their own age were beginning to die. But Mike had resisted treatment, would not take the drugs, hit Jane twice, and three nights ago walked into the VA hospital and cut open his arm in the lobby with a shard of glass.

"They say he hasn't spoken a word," Jane said, as she buckled herself in the backseat. "They can't tell if he's responding to the Ouija board."

Maggie said to Harrison, "That's this blinking light-board, Tom. It's supposed to help balance your brain."

Harrison looked over his shoulder to back out of the drive. "But they think it'll be okay?" he said. "For us all to be there?"

"They think it might help," Maggie said. "They told Jane he needs to see people he knows, people who make him feel safe." She reached back between the seats and took Jane's hand. "Tom's good at that," she said.

Harrison drove in silence and listened to Maggie occupy Jane with questions about EMDR—Eye Movement Desensitization Reprocessing. Maggie once told Harrison that she sometimes forgot that he had been in Vietnam. He wondered whether she was forgetting it now. He and Mike had never talked about Vietnam beyond where and when—Harrison at Dong Ha in 'Sixty-nine, Mike at Pleiku in 'Seventy. Harrison had to question how much comfort he would be to Mike and how much a token of his terrors.

The meeting with Mike went well enough, the doctors said. *Encouraging* was the word that they used. Mike sat in a wheelchair, his left arm bandaged and taped to a board, his face slack, eyes dulled by drugs and roaming the empty cafeteria as though he might at any moment recognize it and break into a panic. Then his chin would fall to his chest and remain there until the male nurse prompted him to "stay with us, Mike."

"I'm going to get better," Mike said at last, as Jane and the nurse wheeled him back to the ward.

"He didn't even know he was crying," Maggie said to Harrison, whose own face felt stuffed with tears. "How could this happen to him, Tom?"

Harrison exhaled deeply and drew a shallow breath. "Let's go wait in the hall," he said.

They took Jane to dinner at a steakhouse none of them knew, and Harrison ordered a second bottle of wine instead of coffee after the meal.

Jane held her cup in both hands and blew absently across the rim. "Can someone really," she said, looking at neither of them, "really come back from something like this. I'm so afraid that he's gone and can never come back."

Maggie and Harrison tried to reassure her, and all three of them accepted the fiction that they were sincere. Maggie counseled time and patience; Harrison spoke of how accomplished psychiatry had become, what wonders the new drugs could do, and of Tom's deep strengths of character.

"They'll let us take the rest of the bottle home, won't they?" Maggie asked, putting her hand over her glass.

Harrison realized he was talking too much and resented Maggie's pointing it out, then, remembering Mike and Jane, felt abashed.

"Sure," he said. "Maybe you'd better drive."

Harrison built houses, and Mike Mitchell had sold them, but their wives socialized more than they did. Harrison could recall only a half-dozen times in fifteen years that he and Mike Mitchell had met for a drink. Things that had seemed innocuous at the time loomed portentous to him now. Once, after Mike had brokered a guarantee for Harrison's first fifty-home tract, they had gone to celebrate at a local college hangout. There among the young men in goatees and shrill coeds in tanktops, beneath the bass guitars bulging from the speakers on the wall, Mike said to Harrison, "They wouldn't last ten minutes in the bush, would they?"

Harrison said he probably wouldn't last ten minutes in that redhead's bush.

Mike laughed and agreed, but he was distant through the rest of their drinks, of which they had too many, though not enough to quell the unease that lay between them.

There had been barbecues and tennis games and dinner parties aplenty over the years, for both couples being childless and middle-aged, they had the time. But Harrison was never drawn to Mike outside that common bond, had, in fact, felt anxious in the knowledge that Mike would like to talk about Vietnam, seemed eager for an opportunity to lapse into a mantra of "they don't know; they weren't there, man," the caricature of an angry vet stalled in frustration. Harrison was troubled that he had not seen this coming, hadn't listened more carefully, hadn't tamped down his own impatience and let Mike vent. He was not one of those, but it wouldn't, he now chided himself, have hurt him to listen.

Before they went to bed that night, while Maggie was in the shower, Harrison took his revolver from the nightstand and emptied the rounds from its cylinder into the waste basket.

The next morning, Harrison picked up paychecks from his accountant and drove to the job site. It was his habit to pay his crews in person, and as his business grew he had especially come to enjoy the task. At least one day a week, he got to speak to everyone who worked for him, call them by their first names, exchange those pleasantries that lubricated their relations. He wanted them—and himself—to remember that he too had started out swinging a hammer. He would still sometimes join a framing crew to stand walls and align top plates. It gave him a simple joy to work with the men. And the fat stack of envelopes in his hand was a measure of how well he was doing.

He parked his pickup and got out at the end of the first of six cul-de-sacs around which his development called Killdeer was rising.

The pneumatic report of the nail gun, its trigger wired back so that it fired each time Fragger shoved its nose against the two-by-four, unexpectedly reminded Harrison of the crack of a carbine, one of those worn-out .30-caliber relics of World War Two, commonplace among the Vietcong, worthless beyond a hundred meters, some cagey Charlie banging away with it from a half-klick out, hoping to draw them in close, where his buddies were crouched in spider holes, ready to pop out and fuck you up but good.

"Fragger," Harrison called to the carpenter, who had stopped to load another strip of nails. "You're working like it's payday." Then, on impulse, he added, "Hell, wind 'em up, Fragger. Everybody's going home early today."

"Hot damn," whooped Fragger, brandishing the nail gun above his head. "A runnin' start on the weekend. You're all right, *daiuy*; I don't care what any of 'em say. Paradise tonight."

Harrison thumbed through the envelopes, pulled one out, and handed it to Fragger.

Fragger kissed the envelope and stuck it upright in the bandana wrapped around his head. "Payday weekend," he said, uncoupling the air hose from the butt of the gun. "Remember what a joke that was in 'nam, *daiuy*?"

"Just barely," said Harrison. "See you on Monday, Fragger."

Harrison had a soft spot for Fragger and the six other sketchy Vietvets on the crew. Their futures were all behind them, and they kept their pasts alive every day in their slang and allusions, even in their names: Fragger, Snooper, Jungle Jim, The Beast. Mike Mitchell had once dropped his bush name: Machinegun Mickey, "as in the mouse," he'd said. But Mike was too near him; "Peers of a par," Maggie had quipped on the golf course one day. And Harrison had no time for any talk of Vietnam that he could not walk away from.

He spent the rest of the morning handing out paychecks, nagged by thoughts of Mike Mitchell and impatient with remembrances of the war that came unbidden, images he could not submerge in the shallow camaraderie of payday.

Wonderboy, the site foreman, was a large, florid man with a full-set of whiskers and a gray-flecked ponytail. He found Harrison in the last cul-de-sac, and they talked for ten minutes about materials and time cards and the sub-contractors scheduled for next week.

"Wonderboy," Harrison said, watching as Fragger's pickup lurched across the muddy job site and onto the street, "tell me something."

"Everything I know," said Wonderboy, "if you've got a minute or two."

"Why is it so many guys like them, so many vets, have never got over 'nam?"

Wonderboy cocked his shaggy head and said, "Shit, cap'n, I don't know. Biggest thing that ever happened to a lot of 'em, I suppose.

And, too, they couldn't sort out how they felt about being a good soldier in a bad war. Fragger, Snooper, some of those guys are still trying to figure it out, I guess. Can't move on until they do."

"Think they ever will?"

"Those guys? Naw. They'll die fighting that war. You have a good weekend, cap'n."

Harrison once read in a local history of the county where his grandparents lived that one of his ancestors had died in 1891 of wounds he received thirty years earlier, at the first Battle of Bull Run. Now it seemed to him that this was what was happening to Mike Mitchell, to Fragger and to Jungle Jim and all the rest. If they didn't die *of* their wounds, they would die around them, like water circling a drain.

Harrison walked woodenly back through the cul-de-sacs, following the curb, his face filled with tears, the way it had been when he saw Mike Mitchell at the hospital. His shoulders trembled, and he felt a pain beneath his collarbone. Angina? he wondered, with only a clinical interest. If I fell dead, he thought, would I care?

The opening in the space that Harrison had put between him and himself filled with those things he refused to remember. He would not recall the times he had been terrified or lethal or set in cold fury. He would not think about throwing up when Black Angus's jaw was shot away or about the howling face that exploded in his rifle sights. He would think about golf, Maggie's breasts, or a white bear.

Harrison walked into the rear bumper of his truck without knowing it was there. He stood bent, massaging his knee, dropping curses like tears, and holding furiously to the image of a white bear.

I'll put the bear in my goddamn knee, he thought. I'll just think about the fucking bear in my knee. Just me, the bear, and my knee. Me, knee, bear. Just the knee. And the goddamn bear. He got stiffly into the truck, still chanting the trinity in his head, and drove without intending it to the blue-collar side of town, coming at last to the Pair-a-

Dice, where Fragger's muddy pickup was parked in the lot. Across one peeling bumper sticker—the likeness of a Bronze Star ribbon—was the legend: "You weren't there!"

Fragger stood with his back to the bar, elbows cocked on it, a beer bottle dangling from his fingers. Fragger had a square jaw and a pot belly and always looked a day behind a shave. He smiled a wide smile as he talked to Snooper, his running mate with the feraldark eyes. Limping, Harrison approached them and soon heard Snooper saying, above the general din of conversation, " ...but it's like I always say, Fragman; you want respect, you got to have it first."

"Semper fi," said Fragger, raising his bottle with a bent wrist.

"Do or die," Snooper said. He drank and smacked his lips.

Fragger saw Harrison and turned toward him, pivoting with one elbow still on the bar. "Hey, *daiuy*," he said. "You come down here to give us our bonus?"

"No," said Harrison, "but I got a tip for you: Don't play the horses. You guys want a beer?"

"Not just one," said Snooper.

"And three shooters of schnapps," Harrison said to the bartender.

After the second round, Harrison didn't know what he was laughing about, only that it was loud and shared by Fragger and Snooper.

"Man, in Dong Ha, we had the worst beer you ever saw," Fragger said. "Some Korean piss. Had so much tin in it, made your fillings hurt."

"Crown," said Harrison, beginning to chuckle again. "Crown beer. I know that shit. Can't trade it for anything."

Harrison realized he had said, "I know," not "I remember."

Snooper said, "I'll never forget the taste of that puke or that fuckin' Australian scotch."

"And," said Fragger, "did you ever get lice, *daiuy*? Like, body lice?"

"Fuck. They sent me down to Da Nang for dysentery, and I came back with goddamn lice," Harrison said. He saw what they were fighting now. These were men locked in mortal combat with loneliness, and for a moment he knew that. Fragger and Snooper had never feared dying, only death. Death was the greatest loneliness, one only hinted at in life by the emptiness we suffer at the death of someone we love. They had lost so many that they knew better than most what loneliness death holds, and only shared memory—volleys of memory—kept it pinned down. But Harrison had never felt that loneliness or that bond. His memories seemed unique to him, except in odd moments like this, and he felt a maudlin wave of companionship curl over him. He was not thinking about the bear in his knee.

"Yeah, I remember lice," he said.

Harrison paid for one more round but left before it came. Two boilermakers and his fresh insight had left him complacent. He was satisfied he had plumbed some universal depth of human understanding, an obscure well of the psyche where knowable demons dwelt.

He noticed his knee when he stepped up into the cab of the truck. The bear was not in it, but Mike Mitchell was. Harrison sat with his hands and forehead on the steering wheel. Perhaps he could have healed Mike's loneliness, or perhaps he would have died of it himself. Either way, didn't he owe Mike that much? Mike hadn't been able to bear the loneliness, because he did not find the equation in which the knowledge of death yields an understanding of love. That was Mike's true despair. That was why he had sounded the alarm.

Harrison felt washed by his love of Maggie and cried at its loneliness, sobbing himself dry in the parking lot, his head and hands on the wheel.

Love in an Election Year

*With thanks to Allison Williams
for permission to borrow from her songs*

When you're blue, it doesn't take a lot to break your heart—a stripped cotton field, a crying child with a dirty face, two raccoons dead by the side of the road—just about everything she'd seen since she left Will in Louisiana. Rosalyn wiped her mouth on her wrist and pushed the bottle of Bushmills back under the seat. Bombay gin and Bushmills were her favorite traveling brands, not that she especially liked them, but those square bottles don't roll out under your brake pedal, yield death on the highway, not that she gave a damn if she did rear-end a combine or impale her Econoline on the spindles of a cotton picker. The banjo tattoo she got to go with Will's mandolin—their pledges in needle, ink, and skin—was still puffed and tender on her shoulder, a taunting reminder that she was bisecting Mississippi on election eve just to put all the miles she could between herself and him in Slidell, rolling desolate back to Knoxville and an empty house whose consolations would be a two-week backlog of mail and maybe Rambler, the semi-independent tomcat she now-and-then fed. But now she couldn't think of Rambler without comparison to Wayward Will and was pissed at herself that he could screw up even her affection for a cat.

Plans are chains, he'd said.

You can't change the plans you haven't made, she said.

It'll all come to me, he said.

Que ser-fuckin-ra? she said.

It will, he said. You need to chill.

Twelve shows in fourteen days, short-circuited sound systems, posters with the wrong dates, house managers who would not be found. But she dealt with it all, updated her Facebook page from cyber cafés and tweeted for the fans. And it *was* fine—riding high on applause at packed shows, melding with Will, his magical mandolin, mountain tenor, and impish smile. His tender attentions. The tattoos had been her idea, and Will was compliant, until she, propped naked in his cousin's extra bed in Slidell, examining her fresh ink, said, "I can't believe we never played together before. We've got to keep this going, Will. Put together another tour, maybe get Chase or Hetty on fiddle. I mean, let's not be too humble: we sound really good together."

Whatever, he said.

This is our time, she said. Now's when we can make this happen—you, me, the music. All we gotta have is a plan.

It'll all come to me, he said. You did.

Sure did, she thought, reaching for the bottle.

Billboards and political posters for candidates she didn't know snapped past like faces in a stranger's photo album, except for one, who had—*damn him*—Will's grin. She studied the signage more closely as it flashed by, but didn't see him again. Her eyes began to bloat with tears.

Easy on the juice, Rosy.

Her iPod had lost its charge, and the discount CD player she put in the van for the tour overheated and skipped. All she could get on the radio was bad Nashville, moldy rock, drive-time ranters, and political promises that didn't reassure her. Rosy began half-humming, half-singing to herself but stopped when she realized they were all songs she and Will had done, played, tried to write. She wanted to think of one that wasn't but couldn't get the others out of her head. *Damn him.* Rosalyn felt usurped, voted out of the office of herself. Even from a hundred miles away, Will could still take up all her space, cast his skinny-assed shadow over everything she cared about—her cat, her music. *I can wreck my own goddamn life,* she thought. *I damn sure don't need him to help me.*

She was on the cusp between sobbing and reaching for the bottle when she saw coming up a wide spot in the road, a bare clapboard store-station-and-café at the intersection of the highway and an unpaved road that ran through the lint-flecked cotton fields into a line of bald cypress. Across from the store was a squat building of concrete block, once painted red, now mottled a dyspeptic pink, windowless and abandoned. She pulled over at the gas pumps, sniffled, blinked, collected herself.

A agéd black man came out the door. In his limp fedora, drab checkered shirt, buttoned to the throat, and shapeless trousers, Rosalyn thought he could have walked out of any decade in the past hundred years—in Mississippi. *Stereotype? Icon? Embalmed history?* She damned Will for her cynicism and swung both feet outside to the ground.

"Hi," she said, mustering all the perk she could gather, as she lifted the nozzle off the pump.

"No 'm," the man said, wagging his head as he approached. "Sign there." He pointed to a hand-lettered notice on the empty towel dispenser between the pumps: "No Self Serve."

"Got no liability, mam. Bes' let me. How much? Fill 'er up?"

She handed him the hose.

"Yeah," she said holding out her key ring. "Thanks. This is the one for the tank. Got cold beer in there?"

"Yes 'm, but befo' noon, you has to ast."

That almost made Rosalyn laugh. *Have to ask. Man.*

The store sold singles, so Rosalyn bought three cans. The fat, slit-eyed woman at the counter put each of them in a small paper sack just its size and then in a larger one with the cheese sticks and peanut-butter crackers.

The man came in and said, "Twenny-fo' sebenty-five on the gas, Miz Bilbo."

The woman nodded without looking at him.

"And I put yo' keys on the seat, mam."

"Thanks," said Rosalyn.

"That your breakfast?" said the woman as she shucked change from the till.

Rosalyn stuffed the bills in her jeans, picked up the sack, and said, "You have a nice day, Miz Bilbo." She gave the pump attendant a dollar as she left.

A quarter-mile from the store, she passed a trooper running radar and was glad that the beer between her legs was still unopened—*damned open-container laws*—and that the Econoline wasn't built for speed. She checked the rearview mirror every few seconds for a mile or more, decided she was cool, and pried open the tab on the can, pausing as she raised it to peek in the mirror one last time and so missed seeing the asphalt welt where the road had been repaired. The van's front tires came off the road on impact, throwing Rosalyn forward, then the rear's hit the welt and snapped her back

There was a squeal of fright from behind her and something struggling among the amps and instruments and duffle bags. Rosalyn's throat froze. She hit the brakes and swerved for the gravel shoulder, squeezing a geyser of beer from the can. Skidding to a halt, she slammed the transmission into park, jumped out, and ran to the cargo door on the other side, her mind a mess as she slid it open and cocked the half-crushed can in its soggy sack like a rock, ready to stone whatever was inside.

Finding her voice in a spark of confidence (she hadn't been jumped yet), she screamed, "Who the fuck are you? Get the fuck out of my van. Now."

Something stirred beneath the moving-blanket that doubled as the van's mattress, and a girl's trembling voice said, "Don't hurt me. Please. I'm gettin' out."

She was fifteen or sixteen, plain, narrow hipped, her dark hair tipped in purple. Like Rosalyn, she was dressed in jeans and a cotton sweater, though hers was decorated with out-sized safety pins. She held a small backpack to her chest and looked at the ground.

Her adrenaline abated, Rosalyn tossed the can in a shock of dead sumac and said, "What the fuck are you doing? You scared the holy shit out of me."

"I'm sorry," said the girl. "I just need a ride, is all."

"You could have *asked* me for a ride, girl."

"No 'm. No, I couldn't. If she'd have seen me, she wouldn't have let me go."

"Who?"

"Aunt Doris."

"Would that be Miz Bilbo?"

The girl nodded and glanced up. The corners of her lips quivered.

"You know her?"

"Look—what's your name, anyway?"

"Dierdre."

"Look, Dierdre, my name's Rosy, and I know you have your reasons, sweetheart, but I can't be transporting a runaway."

"I'm not running away," Dierdre said. "In fact, I'm going to see my mother up in Starkville."

"And your aunt wouldn't like that why?"

"It's all right," Dierdre said as she put her arms through the pack straps. "It's okay. I'll be okay. Just don't tell anybody you seen me. Okay?"

Rosalyn was strongly of two or three minds. The girl stirred deep sympathies in her—Rosalyn had been the runaway once and luckier among strangers than others she knew. There was a freight of bad juju in the world for a girl like Dierdre, whose pleading, fear-pried eyes were wild with sadness. But Rosalyn had trouble enough in mind, didn't need to be pulled over, reeking of spilt beer, with a teenage truant in tow. And she wasn't at all sure she wanted to put her own sorrows aside for someone else's. She wasn't through with them yet. Couldn't she even have her sadness to herself? Did she have to be heartbroken for somebody else, too?

There's a song in every story, Rosy. Isn't that what you always say? If it's a good song, it doesn't have to be worth the heartbreak.

"Kiss my dead dog," she said. "Get in before they come looking for you."

Dierdre sat in the passenger seat and stared down the road while Rosalyn peeled off her beery sweater and jeans and changed into fresh clothes from a duffle bag in the back.

"You owe me some laundry, girl," she said as she wheeled back onto the two-lane blacktop.

"I'm sorry. I'm really sorry. Thank you. Thank you for taking me. I'll pay you back. I promise."

"Shouldn't make promises you don't mean to keep, Miss Dierdre—is it Bilbo?"

"No." She snarled the word and at once said, "I'm sorry. I know you didn't mean nothing. It's Wicket. Kids call me Dierdre Wicked or Wicked Wicket. They think I'm a Goth."

"You are?"

"I don't know. I guess."

"But Miz Bilbo doesn't like it."

124

"I don't think she gives a shit what I do. Uncle Eli's the one who ... well ...."

"What? He whip you?"

"He wanted to see if I got any tattoos. Anywhere."

"Oh, hell, sweetheart, did he ... ?"

"No. But he's going to. If I'd stay there, he would."

"You can put the sonofabitch in jail. Right now."

Dierdre shook her head.

"No," she said. "No. I just wanna see my mother in Starkville. I get to Starkville, things'll be okay."

"There's string-cheese and crackers in that bag, if you're hungry."

Dierdre put the bag in her lap.

"Can I have a beer?" she said

In for a penny, in for a pound. "Seeing that's all we've got. Give me one, too. And a pack of crackers."

They drove in silence for a while, eating and drinking. As they passed a house with a cross in the yard and an American flag and the Stars and Bars flying from the porch, Dierdre put her face between her knees.

"Know somebody there?" Rosalyn said.

Dierdre sat up. "Aunt Doris's creepy preacher. He's the one first ast Uncle Eli about my tattoos. Said maybe I's a satanist."

"Mmm. So, Dierdre, tell me: what's the story? You're down here, mother's up in Starkville, uncle's a letch, aunt won't let you go. What's all that?"

"Nothing. It's all a buncha bullshit."

"C'mon, girl. There's nothing on the radio, and we got lots of miles to go to get to where we're going."

"You some kind of musician, aren't you? What do you play?"

"Banjo, mostly. Some guitar. I sit in on bass once in a while."

"I mean, what kind of music?"

"Oh. Old-time, mountain music, jug band. You know, hillbilly music."

"Oh. I'm gonna play lead guitar someday."

"But you were saying about your life as you already know it...."

It was like picking bad stitches from a seam, but mile by mile Rosalyn teased out threads of Dierdre's story: raised around Gulfport and Biloxi, only child of an itinerant-bartender mother and long-absent father, already twice a drop-out, sent to live with an aunt and uncle in the country when her mother said she couldn't handle her any more. The last Dierdre heard from her was a phone call a month ago to say she was leaving bad luck behind and heading up to Starkville.

"What's she do in Starkville?" Rosalyn said.

Dierdre shrugged, sucked on her empty beer can. "She never said. Bar tending, probably." Dierdre shut one eye and peered into the can's vent. "But, you know, I know she loves me. She's just had a hard life is all. Know what I mean?"

"Oh, yeah. It's not all happy childhoods."

"No shit."

Still, Rosalyn realized, *only a pang. Lord, how fast heartbreak dwindles to humdrum pain. How strange, almost perverse, that someone else's hurt can water-down your own.*

She felt ashamed of herself and looked down the road, checking out each cluster of campaign signs, hoping to see Will's smile again, test the mettle of her sorrow.

"You got any cigarettes?" Deirdre said.

"Nope, and no smoking in Vroom Hilda."

"Jeez. What's that? A name? Vroom Hilda?"

"Old comic strip. You're too young to know it."

"I *guess.*"

Rosalyn felt stung, dated, and at the same time frustrated by a spark of impatience with the girl, with seeing in her one word a smart-mouthed pain in the ass.

Easy, Rosy. Easy on her. We all have our reasons.

"Hey," she said, "I just thought: you know how to get in touch with your mother once we get to Starkville?"

"I got her address off a letter she sent Aunt Doris. She got an apartment."

"And you have it with you."

"Yesss," Dierdre said. "Is that all you're gonna do, ast me questions?"

"I guess I could let you walk from here."

Dierdre squirmed and stared at the passing roadside.

Rosalyn let the silence linger. She knew how it would go. Everything about Will that made her crazy—his casual arrogance, his allergy to ambition, his languid immobility—would start to fade, and more vividly she would recall the crowds and bottles and beds they'd shared. She might even finish one of the songs they started to write. There'd be a campaign of her heart against her head, Dionysus versus Apollo, justifications and rationalizations wrestling for her soul. She knew. It wasn't her first goat-ropin'. But she'd tried love with the well-adjusted, and they left almost no memories, none that swelled toward song, at least, toward that life more abundant. Was it not love unless it could leave you an oil slick on the floor? She hoped she didn't *need* men who'd ruin her life just to have one worth living.

They made a pit stop in Philadelphia, and over the tacos that Rosalyn sprang for, she said, "I've got a cell phone in the van, Dierdre. You want to try information, see if your moms has a phone listed?"

Dierdre slurped through her soda straw and looked up.

"You got a cell? Cool."

"Hang on. I'll go get it."

Rosalyn got the number for a Molly Wicket in Starkville, confirmed the address, and gave the phone and the napkin with the number on it to Dierdre.

"Can I take this back to the ladies' room?" Dierdre said. "I don't wanna talk with all these people around."

"Go for it. Want anything for the road?"

"Coke."

Rosalyn wondered whether she'd ever see her phone again, whether Will could work spooky action at a distance, cause others, too, to wander.

Minutes later, Dierdre came back smiling, rolling on the balls of her feet as she walked.

"You talk to her?" Rosalyn said.

"Got her answering machine. She's there, all right."

It was less than an hour to Starkville, and Dierdre filled a lot of it caroming from happy memories about days beach-combing and collecting shells to dreams of having her own band, when she got good enough, getting a job, going to college in Starkville. Rosalyn appreciated the effervescence, that it left her own heart leaden.

The apartment building was a vinyl-sided, two-story rectangle on the fringe of what Rosalyn took to be the student ghetto. The apartments opened directly onto common walkways. Rosalyn and Dierdre climbed the rusty stairs to 210, knocked, and waited.

"Look," said Dierdre, "I know I've been kind of a shit, but I really, really appreciate what you've done, Rosy. Really. And you don't have to stick around. I can just wait here until my mom gets home."

"That's okay. Let's ask some of the neighbors, see if we can find out where she is."

A woman two doors down came out with a small dog on a leash and as she was sorting through her key ring said, "If you're looking for that one, better try the jail."

"Jail?" said Dierdre.

"What for?" Rosalyn said. "What happened?"

"Two nights ago. Took her and some man away. That's all I know."

"Not again, Mama. No," said Dierdre.

Oh, shit, Rosalyn thought, but she said, "Dierdre, don't get upset, sweetie. Not yet. Let's go find out what's up."

A few phone calls and a short drive had them at the police station where Dierdre's mother was being held, and the uniformed woman at the desk had to come from behind it to calm Dierdre, who, even after she finally sat down, clutching her backpack to her like a stuffed toy, kept repeating, "Where is she? Where have you got my mother?"

Rosalyn answered the officer's questions as best she could. After a few minutes, the woman went to a glass partition behind her and spoke through a grille to another officer who came out and said, "Dierdre Wicket? Leave your pack with the sergeant there and come with me. I'll take you to see your mother."

"What's the charge?" Rosalyn said as Dierdre and the jailer disappeared through a door.

"Possession with intent to deliver."

"Drugs?"

"Uh-huh."

"And what about Dierdre?"

"Thought you was just a good Samaritan givin' the girl a ride. What do you care?"

"Look, please, just tell me what's going to happen to her, okay?

"That's up to social services."

"They can't send her back to that aunt and uncle. He's going to, to *interfere* with that girl, don't you understand?"

The officer looked at Rosalyn then past her through the double glass doors to the parking lot.

"That your van out there?"

"Yes."

"And you transported her from where?"

"South of Philadelphia. I told you that. Listen, the situation back at her aunt and uncle's is, well, it's unhealthy. Uncle's got his hands all over her, and the aunt couldn't care less."

"You sure know a lot about somebody you just met. How much more are you not saying? Maybe you know a lot, maybe you took her outta that unhealthy situation. You maybe think you're the good Samaritan, mam, but kidnappin's a serious offense."

"I didn't kidnap anyone. I just gave the girl a ride. Look, would it do any good for me to talk to social services?"

"Prob'ly not. You're not friend nor kin, now, are you?"

Rosalyn began to tremble with anger and impotent grief, and she knew she had to walk away before she made things worse.

She found a parking place on an empty side street and sat there crying into her hands. She felt that everything was her fault, that she should have done something more for Dierdre, that she had failed Will, that that was what she did: failed people, herself, her music. It was a half-hour before she could start the van and drive out of Starkville.

Back on the open road, her carry-out coffee fortified with Bushmills, Rosalyn could think again. She knew things weren't really her fault, and someday she'd probably believe that. Someday. But that someday still wouldn't know how to deal with joy and sorrow today. Why is it, she wondered, that joys in their time never seem as intense as sorrows? But, then, why are they better remembered, come to mean more to life? Because sorrow is too crushing to live with? But joy can be borne, if only because it is so fleeting? And what do we do then? What do we do when the sorrow's gone but the light of joy's fading? We keep trying to go there again, rekindle it, keep falling in love, writing songs, adopting stray cats.

She heard a fresh tune in her head and snatches of lyrics:

> *Crossing Mississippi in November,*
> *cotton fields all stripped and falling apart,*

all the something something something something
just the things I need to break my heart.

Rambler, she thought, *we got us work to do, Mister Whiskers.*
Thank God, there's work for us to do.

Tasting Notes

Dickie Watkins was, in fact, of fully average stature, but he did not see himself so. Rooms expanded to dwarf him when he walked in; people swelled like funhouse grotesques. And when he heard others inflating themselves with their opinions and anecdotes, Dickie retreated into his world of wines, silently chanting his life list of exotic vintages, the first-growth French grand crus and obscure primitivos of the Italian boot heel. As Master of the Cellar at Blackchiefs Shore Island Golf and Country Club, he had learned to navigate the conversational shallows of land values and fairway woods, but he knew that he was truly himself only with wines and those who loved them. That he had once mistaken Trudy Phillips for one of them was an abiding reminder of how little he understood of the world above the cellar. He cringed at the memory of his brief crush on her, sour now as green grapes between his teeth.

"Dickie, you silly wanker," Trudy said, unfurling her arm in an arc that ended with her cocktail glass extended, shoulder high, "look up here and listen to me. I said, there's a bottle of that yummy Château Margaux on the auction list at Vivendi's."

"Not the 'Sixty-six," said Dickie.

"Of course it's the 'Sixty-six," said Trudy, crossing her legs as she turned fully toward him on her barstool. "Whatever else could we be talking about, you silly wanker? Don't you just know it's all luscious with horehound and civet by now?"

"I didn't know there was one left on the island," Dickie said. "You're sure it's the 'Sixty-six?"

"Rudi— you do know Rudi, don't you? Vivendi's new maître d'? – Rudi said it's probably the last one south of Charleston."

"And probably well past its prime," said Dickie, as he mentally calculated whether he could afford what a bottle of Château Margaux 'Sixty-six ought to fetch at Vivendi's cellar auction.

"Well, for God's sake, Dickums, it's not going to get any younger. Besides, I had a bottle of it last summer in Bath, and it was just gorgeous, completely wolverine."

"You're . . . you . . . you're not going to bid for it, are you?"

"With that bastard Bob Phillips' next alimony check." Trudy smiled over the rim of her glass. "It'll be the best thing he's given me since the divorce."

The thought of Trudy and her ex-husband glaring at each other as they waved their bidders' cards above their heads, jacking the price of the Margaux through the high ceiling of Vivendi's dining room, caused Dickie to contract with alarm. Worse, he imagined Trudy winning the bid, slurping a 'Sixty-six Margaux, and pronouncing it the essence of puma. He felt tractionless as a jellyfish on the beach.

"Oh," he said, "oh, I wouldn't do that, Trudy. It would be such a terrible waste. Of money, I mean. I'm sure it's, well, too *civety* by now."

"Pooh," Trudy said. "It's not my money. But now you must tell me, Dickums, do you have some really yummy ones for us tonight? Something all fish market and buckthorn?"

"Oh, yes," Dickie said. "I'm sure there's something you will like." He poured his club soda down his throat and said that he really should go see that the spittoons were on the tables.

In the few steps down the hall from the bar to the ballroom, Dickie set his mind back on the tasting and felt a rising calm as he walked in and shut the double doors behind him. Inside the Blackchiefs ballroom, tasting tables ringed the dance floor, each one draped in damask cloths overlapped to form diamonds of silver and gold. Upon each table stood a rank of wine bottles masked in paper sleeves, a field of stemmed glasses, and next to a stoneware spittoon the size of a Jeroboam, a bowl of oyster crackers and a fan of paper napkins embossed with the Blackchiefs seal. On the bandstand a young woman with long, black hair sat before a grand piano practicing soft runs, while a loose herd of waiters milled nearby, lowing quietly and smoothing the napkins draped over their arms. Dickie suffered a slight contraction as he approached them.

"Mister Dickie," said Morgan, the headwaiter, "ever'thing is ready, suh. And if you don't mind my sayin', this selection here tonight is just super. In fact, you ask me, this is goin' to be your best tastin' ever."

Dickie enlarged a fraction, enough to say, "Thank you, Morgan," before he veered away, as though repelled by an invisible shield, and began fiddling with the numbered sleeves on the bottles, sinking back in funk at the thought of Trudy Phillips sucking from a bottle of Château Margaux 'Sixty-six.

Dickie cocked his head as the pianist played the right hand to "Heart and Soul," letting each note hang and almost die before she played the next. He wondered whether musicians ever played without hearing each note, experiencing the song as a single thing, beyond the sum of its parts, as he did with wines when they sang on his tongue. He felt the nip of his frustration with wine writers, whose feeble appeals to nose and palate, those rote and superficial descriptives, struck him as almost mathematically abstract. He could speak in the received vocabulary of wine connoisseurs as well as anyone, but his own attempts at written reviews always ended thrashing in musical metaphors. He could not imagine how wines tasted to Trudy Phillips.

The pianist stopped. Dickie slipped a gold railroad watch from his vest pocket and called to the waiters, "It's time, gentlemen. You may open the doors now, Morgan."

As the waiters took their places around the room, Dickie gave it a final sweep, making sure the placards identifying each table's range of selections were easily seen, to spare the embarrassment of anyone (like Trudy Phillips) who couldn't tell a Burgundy from a Russian River sewage spill. Then he let his eyes linger at the table designated "Tasters' Test." On it stood an imposing row of ten bottles, ranging from a first-growth Bordeaux grand cru to some mildewed Chilean plonk he had bought at a convenience store, its vintage the previous week. He thought of it now with Trudy in mind. Dickie Watkins liked a joke as well as anyone.

At Dickie's nod, the pianist commenced a lush rendition of "My Favorite Things," and the members began to drift from the bar into the ballroom. Dickie waited for the crowd to gather then stepped onto the bandstand and spoke into the side of the microphone there, as though whispering in someone's ear.

"Good evening, ladies and gentlemen, and welcome to Reds of the World. We have a gala selection this evening–our headwaiter has already declared it 'super'"—Morgan bowed to the cheerful applause—"so I know you all want to get started. I'll see the more intrepid among you at the 'Tasters' Test' at"—he glanced down at his watch—"at seven-thirty. Until then, enjoy. But remember: no peeking, and don't forget to spit."

The crowd responded with an obligatory chuckle and began sorting itself among the tables.

Dickie poured himself a half-glass of a Côte du Rhône he was fond of and circulated behind the arc of tables, occasionally smiling and raising his glass to someone in the crowd, always with one eye out for Trudy Phillips.

Astrid "Trudy" Phillips, née Hapgood, was the soi-disant doyenne of Dickie Watkins' fans and protégées, but there was nothing he could do about it. It was her ex-husband, Bob Phillips, Secretary of the Governing Board of Blackchiefs, who had lured him away from the wage-slave gentility of Vivendi's Fine Dining and created the post of

Master of the Cellar just for Dickie, who enjoyed a member's privileges while charging tuition for the wine-appreciation classes that he taught—and taught with such a modest erudition that they had come into perpetual vogue among the wives, first among them Trudy.

She was wearing fitted, puce cashmere the night that Bob Phillips introduced him to the club, here in this same ballroom, set up much as it was tonight for Blackchiefs' first taste of Dickie's art. The men were all in tuxedos for it, and the women, save for Trudy, all wore evening gowns.

"I'm Trudy Phillips," she had said, extending her hand, "and I know who you are, Dickie Watkins. At Vivendi's, don't you remember?"

"Of course," he said. "Missus Phillips."

"Trudy. Call me Trudy. Bob said you'll be offering classes soon. Is that right?"

"Do you enjoy wines?"

Her laugh even then was bold, but not yet gone to brass. "At least in quantity," she said conspiratorially. "Show me something really good."

Dickie did, and she hung both on his words and his shoulder as he took her from table to table, offering samples of some of his favorites, while he expanded and contracted in a welter of unaccustomed sensations. Trudy Phillips was not an unattractive woman—far from it: her wrists were slim and her voice had a broad timbre that he took for monied confidence—but did she have to stand so close to him, her slender fingers familiar with his lapels? She would, however, lapse into a thoughtful silence as he spoke of the wine he was pouring her, sip it, and declare herself amazed.

Dickie was not immune to these attentions. He enjoyed the enlarged sense of himself he felt under her appreciative gaze, but he shriveled beneath the knowledge that she was his patron's wife and nearly passed to invisibility at the thought of Bob Phillips casting him out in a fit of jealous rage. Trudy straightened his tie. Perhaps, he thought, this was just the custom of their crowd.

Later that evening, after Trudy had freed Dickie to circulate for some time among the tasting tables and trays of canapés, she found him detailing the vagaries of cultivating the pinot noir. His small knot of auditors included her husband, who looked pleased as a man who had discovered a rare print at a flea market.

"Oh, Bob," Trudy said, "you can't go on monopolizing like this. Let him have some air."

She took Dickie's arm and marched him out the French doors onto the verandah, where fireflies winked in the mellow air. She steered him to the parapet overlooking the eighteenth green of the Hurricane Course, the bald cypress along its rough like darker shadows of the night. Trudy rested her elbows on the stone coping and stared past the trees, breathing deeply through her nose. It was a moist and velvet night, moonless and warm, and Dickie was deep in appreciation of it—and for the moment genuinely pleased with his place in life—when Trudy turned and kissed him wetly on the corner of his mouth and said: "You are a genius, Dickie Watkins. And we are so lucky to have you."

Dickie recoiled as from a slap and compressed himself into something that would slide through a barrel bung. Taking her hand as he shrank away, Dickie said, "Well, yes. It's my p-privilege."

She tugged him toward the door, impatient now as a mother with a dawdling child. "Oh, come on then," she said. "It was just a little kiss."

Dickie paused by the bandstand to survey the ballroom. Intimidated? he thought. No, not by this room full of his intimates, this congregation of old friends, for he knew every wine in the room, and they, in turn, rewarded him with their full realm of experiences. Some, like the Rhône in his hand, were familiar and reassuring; the potent

New World zinfandels inspired conviviality; while others, like the grand cru on the Tasters' table, were complex as chess, deep as the emotions . . . of song.

He was rapt in the pianist's chorus of "Fly Me to the Moon," when Trudy Phillips' voice yanked him from his reverie.

"Dickie," she said loudly. She waved her glass above her head and surged toward him through the crowd.

He locked a smile on his lips as she threw her weight on one hand and leaned across the table between them. "Oh, Dickums," Trudy said, "I've never tasted so much pitchblende and tartar in one room. They're all so, so lubricant."

"Well, yes," said Dickie, thinking of the vernacular Chilean and now certain why he must have bought it. "There's one over there somewhere in the middle of the Tasters' table that I know you will just love."

He cast a glance toward Morgan, hoping to catch his eye. "Oh, Morgan needs something," he said. "Mustn't let Morgan fret."

The memory of that single kiss had lingered on Dickie's cheek, as did the scent of Trudy's perfume on his tuxedo jacket, well into his first series of classes. When she wasn't casting sly, knowing smiles at him, Trudy was attentive, taking notes and sipping and spitting with studious gravity. But as the lessons progressed, Dickie saw a frown of disaffection sometimes wrinkle Trudy's brow as she swirled the wine in her mouth, searching for those elusive flavors he described—the banana in a Beaujolais, the pepper in a pinot. She smiled less at him, and her look of perplexity soon turned to impatience, and eventually to vexation. They were about halfway through the evening on Iberian reds, he recalled, when Trudy suffered her crisis.

Dickie had taught himself to whistle (approximately) the word "parakeet," and was doing so in his description of the Portuguese grape of that name, to the delight of the half-dozen wives in the class, when

Trudy, who most definitely had not been spitting, barked out, "Hell, Dickie, they all taste like buckthorn and asafetida."

Horror hung in the silence that followed. Glasses froze in midsip; throats contracted; and Dickie stood rooted in shock, red with embarrassment for Trudy.

Trudy, for her part, leaned back in the sofa, crossed her legs, spun her glass, and said, "But, of course, its tooth of meniscus does carry a bite of hedgehog and wolverine."

The women tittered, and Dickie went on, but the atmosphere was poisoned.

Worse was later, when she got him alone. "God bless you, Dickie Watkins," she said to him. "I can taste it now; the scales are falling from my tongue. So to speak."

Many later suspected that it was the trouble in her marriage that made Trudy change, but for whatever reason, she was never the same after that. She began making expansive tasting notes in her small tablet, even of the Club House vin ordinaire, and took up the habit of appearing from nowhere to hook her hand over Dickie's shoulder and declare at large: "Hedgeapple, kelp, and sumac for the fruits; bait shop, asafetida, and wolverine for the rest, once you get past the grape. Isn't that right, Dickums?"

After that, Dickie sent his jacket to be cleaned, and he shaved his cheek more closely.

The pianist moved into a bright, percussive version of "Tea for Two," and Dickie stood by the Saint Emilion table to listen, wondering whether anyone had singled out the off-year Château Beauséjour-Duffau. Morgan, who was filling water glasses on the apron of the bandstand, said, "You stumped 'em good tonight, Mister Dickie. There's two gentlemen over by the Coat Doo Bone nearly come to blows already."

Dickie sipped his wine, letting it harmonize with the pianist's wistful improvisation, a juxtaposition of unanticipated delight, when Trudy's voice fell on his ear like a clinker.

"Dickie. Dickie. Over here."

Trudy plowed through the crowd, a pastel ice-breaker towing a small, elderly man with a tobacco-stained mustache. He tugged his sleeve free, smoothed his lapels and his mustache, touched Trudy's arm, and disappeared back into the crowd. Trudy stood on tiptoe to look for him, then resumed her progress toward the Saint Emilion.

"Dickie, you awful wanker, don't you run away too. You've got to hear what Doctor Jenks just said about the Napas."

Dickie braced himself, holding out a glass of water as Trudy made the table.

"No, no," she said, waving her hand. "None of that, Dickums. Listen to this: Doctor Jenks says that the character of the Napas is ruled by undertones of smegma and sloughed skins. Isn't that pernicious?"

"Perfectly. They're also 'degenerate parvenus' and 'barbecue antidotes,' I think I've heard him say. Doctor Jenks does know his opinions."

Not calling for the waiter, Trudy poured herself a generous measure from the bottle nearest at hand and drank it down in a swallow. "I know," she said, as she slipped toward the next table. "And he's so vivid in them. Entirely fish market."

In June, just after her divorce and on the night before she left for England to take the cure at Bath, Trudy Phillips excused herself from her dinner companions and stole down the service stairs into the Blackchiefs wine cellar, where Dickie was cataloging a shipment of vouvrays and pasting their labels on the racks where they would rest, briefly, from their long voyage at sea.

"Dickie?" she said sotto voce.

Dickie looked up from the invoice, feeling exposed without his jacket and with his cuffs turned up.

"I'm over here," he said. "Among the whites." He was irritated to find himself echoing her cathedral hush, and he added distinctly, "That's to your left."

Trudy appeared in the narrow aisle between the ceiling-high racks, goggling like a tourist, her clutch purse held in both hands across her chest. "Oh, Dickums," she said, "I've never been down here before. All it needs are cobwebs and a suit of rusty armor."

"It's not a dungeon," he said, "or a tomb. There's no need to whisper."

Trudy looked at him and said, "Of course it isn't, silly. What ever made you think so?"

The shadows thrown on her face by the frosted light of the ceiling fixtures made her look equal parts coquette and mad woman, each equally disconcerting to Dickie.

"You're leaving us tomorrow, aren't you?" he said, pasting up another label.

"And you, Dickie, are the only one I'll really miss."

Dickie turned to her, hoping his head would sink inside his chest.

She fumbled in her clutch purse and withdrew a small, oblong package wrapped in gift paper. Handing it to him, she said, "Your friendship has meant everything these past few weeks."

Dickie was stunned by this declaration: he had seen Trudy hardly at all since the news of her pending divorce became public. And he counted himself, at best, indulgently civil toward her.

"No," he said. "No, really. That's . . . it's not . . . ."

Trudy's already wan smile faded to a moue of exasperation.

"Take the damn present, Dickums."

"Yes," he said. "Thank you."

He peeled off the paper and opened the box inside to find a double-curved wine key, its ebony handle inlaid with his initials in sterling.

"For you," Trudy said, "for what you've taught me–the appreciation of something larger than myself. I can't take a sip of wine, Dickie, without thinking of you, you and those yummy flavors I never knew before. Who would have thought there was so much horehound in merlot?"

Pretending to admire the wine key, Dickie stared at the floor drain and wished that he could swirl down it. *Mint and menthol,* he wanted to shout at her. Instead he thanked her again and praised the lines of the key, its heft and balance.

"Now, Dickums," Trudy said, "you must tell me about this English wine, this claret that I'll be drinking."

By seven-thirty, Dickie had made his way around the tables and took up a position at the Tasters' Test beside Morgan, whom he had asked to help him pour. The crowd was already three-deep, with Trudy occupying the center of the first rank.

"Dickie," she said, waggling her wine glass at him, "do you think that zinfandels have socialist tendencies?"

Dickie cleared his throat and raised his right hand as though taking an oath. "Ladies and gentlemen," he said, "excuse me. What we have here are ten wines from across the spectrum of worldly–and not so worldly–reds, from the finest to the foul. So, cleanse your palates and let's see who can tell the difference."

Morgan passed his palms above the bottles like a virtuoso of the theramon and smiled at the eddy of faces. "What'll be your pleasures, ladies and gentlemen?"

Trudy held out her glass. "Number one, to begin," she said.

Dickie had the knack of looking sidelong, so while appearing not to do so, he kept his eye on Trudy as she swirled and made faces and jotted her tasting notes, swallowing with an exaggerated thrust of her chin. Trudy kept her notes on a small calf-bound tablet with a pocket in the spine for a slim, gold pen that she worried with her teeth as she chose her descriptives. Dickie sniffed the corks lying behind the bottles, found the grand cru between the Chilean and a South African syrah, then settled into smallness to await Trudy's reaction.

Like a gambler with a system, Trudy moved methodically from end to end of the row of bottles, working her way toward the center. Dickie was humming with excitement as she approached it. He saw her cock one eyebrow as she swished the Jo'burg syrah, then he had to wait in suspense while she scrawled in her tablet before asking Morgan to pour her the Chilean.

No sooner had the wine passed Trudy's lips than she puckered her cheeks, popped her eyes, and spewed a stream of something like tar in the general direction of the spittoon.

"God damn, Dickie," she said, the crowd drawing back from her as she raked off the last of her lipstick with a napkin. "What the hell is that, syrup of ipecac?"

"With pine tar and marmot urine," said Dickie, who felt fit to burst, despite his mild disappointment that the others would likely forego the Chilean. "Very nicely done."

Morgan, meanwhile, his dignity unfazed, threw a fresh napkin over the stain and removed the spattered glasses. He handed Trudy a fresh one and said, "Maybe a taste of number five, Miz Trudy?"

The crowd closed around her as Morgan poured. Trudy held her glass to the light and tilted the wine up the side.

"Purple as an old bruise," she said. "Hematoma with legs."

Trudy lowered the glass and held it to her nose. The crowd fell silent, and even Dickie felt a frisson of anticipation.

A smile spread across Trudy's lips. "Wet earth," she said. "Something over-ripe, like dark roses or sphagnum peat."

Dickie shook his head and put a finger in his ear to clear it: he could hardly believe the words came from Trudy: there was song in her voice. She put the glass to her lips and slubbered the wine between them, then held her head back—like a dove, Dickie thought, like a dove—and swallowed.

Trudy's face softened, glowed with the mild, warm light of a saint in ecstasy.

"Bramble fruit," she said throatily. "Iron and nicotine." She slid one hip on the table and leaned sideways across it toward Dickie. "Barnyard and sweet William," she said.

A moment enveloped Dickie Watkins and Trudy Phillips, expanding until it excluded all else.

"Plums," Dickie said, whistling the ess low and long.

"Black walnut," Trudy said from deep in her throat.

Dickie took the glass from her hand and drank, putting his lips where her lips had been.

"Root and vine," he said, putting one knee on the table. He reached for her and she came to him.

"It was always for us, Dickie," she said in his ear. "The Margaux 'Sixty-six, it was always for us."

The pianist played the melody to "Lush Life" with both hands.

"Anyone else?" Morgan said.

North Star

This is how it was told to me when I was young.

Long ago when there were trolls, they all lived under bridges. The trolls were cruel and feared, even by their own kind, and so they had been driven from the warm realms of men. The last trolls that remained, then, were in the cold, distant northern lands like savage Nova Zembla, where the Ice Princess ruled the short summer thaw.

Through ten months of winter, the trolls slept snug in caves beneath their bridges, and the Ice Princess lay on a bed of ice in a castle of ice so cold that it was blue. When herdsmen brought their reindeer north to pasture in the spring, the trolls awoke to the sound of hooves clattering on their wooden bridges. And they were hungry trolls after their long sleep. They stole the reindeer and fought away the wolves, and if the herdsman were very young or very old, they might drag him off too. The Princess did not care. She walked abroad in the land she ruled with a heart as cold as a slice of midnight moon. The summer was too short to warm her heart through and through, so like her castle it would not melt before the early snows returned.

There was one troll, the last one ever born and so the youngest of them all, who was not like the rest. He too carried off the herdsmen's stock, for every troll must eat, but he could not take a man or understand why they cursed him in their strange speech. He only did what was always done in that distant land of ice: he ate the meat of the herdsmen's deer to warm his cold insides. And the thought that that was all there was made him sad. No troll had ever thought this way before. But no troll had ever known love. All their warmth came from what they ate and the flush of fighting wolves. Nor did the youngest troll call it love: he did not know what it was. He knew only that he had a place inside that was never warm however much he ate or fought. Feeling this, he went one spring to find the Princess whom, though he did not know it, no troll had ever seen. He wanted her to give him back the fierce peace of mind that every troll should know.

The Princess rose from her bed of ice and rubbed the frost from her eyes. Out the frozen pane of the window in her room, she saw her twin sentry eagles had thawed, were rising stiffly from the towers of her castle keep. So the Princess went to walk her land. Her pale, rich gown reached to the ground and trailed frost stars in her wake. The nubby grass turned brown where she had passed. Her eagles soared above her.

The troll, meanwhile, had bathed himself in the cold stream beneath his bridge, gnawed short the long, yellow nails on his toes and fingers, and brushed his tangled fur with a stem of briar. He waited anxiously in a thicket where he hoped the Princess might pass. He held a fresh haunch of reindeer to give to her to show he meant no harm. Suddenly, she appeared over a low hill nearby, her eagles circling high overhead, the grass withering behind her.

"Majesty," said the troll, stepping from the thicket and holding the reindeer haunch in his outstretched hands. "A favor, Your Majesty, a small favor. No one else may help me. Take this food and be kind."

She looked at him, and her eyes were like two knives of ice. "What are you, troll?" she said. "Do you dare to look at me? Do you want my eagles to take your eyes that you may never find your cave again?"

The troll looked down at his hairy feet, but a picture of the Princess' pale beauty stayed in his mind, and he grew less cold inside.

148

"My gift, Majesty," he said and offered her the meat.

"Give it to my birds," she said. "They eat for me."

He cast the meat on the ground near the Princess where the two eagles, now pacing about like crows, attacked it with their beaks,

"Now, troll," the Princess said, "kneel and speak, but be brief."

"Majesty, I have a cold place inside that will not go away."

"That is your heart, troll."

"Then have your birds peck it out."

The Princess narrowed her eyes and looked at the troll's bowed head. "I do not understand you, troll. I think you must be evil."

"Majesty," the troll said, "that's to say that water's wet and the sky's above."

The Princess eyes narrowed more. "You know of evil, then, troll?"

"It is a word men use that I do know."

"Then you are indeed a strange troll, and I never want to see you again. It is well you are the last born of your kind. Nova Zembla was never meant to know the ways of men, and especially not such an exceedingly ugly troll."

The troll stood, trembling and staring at his hairy feet, until he heard the eagles flap away. When he looked up, the Princess' frost-bitten path broke over the hill, and she was out of sight.

The troll was deeply hurt by what the Princess said, but when he thought of her, a tingling warmth squeezed the cold inside him to a thin chill and longing. Each time he hunted and crossed her barren path, he put his nose to the ground to see whether the track were fresh. Each time it was he followed it, hoping for another glimpse of the Princess, but the sight of the soaring eagles kept him away. By the time the first frost came, he had a plan.

When winter roared down from the pole, and the eagles were frozen fast to their tower battlements, the troll stole into the castle of ice and carried the Princess off to his cave. There they slept the winter through, curled like two spoons in a box, the warmth of the troll melting the Princess' heart.

The herdsmen came early that year. The troll awoke and saw the Princess still curled in the shape of a spoon, the shape of his long dreams, the shape of the warmth that filled him. There were tiny lines around her eyes now, lines frozen flesh had never known. The troll felt a wetness on his cheeks but did not know to call it tears. He went to find food for the Princess' first meal.

The Princess awoke soon after the troll had gone. She was startled at first to find no frost sealing her eyes, but she was unafraid. A feeling she had never known flowed through her. She quickly brushed the leaves and grass from her silver gown and stepped, blinking, from the mouth of the cave. The soft breezes of the thaw filled her with warmth, She leaped to the bank of the stream and looked over all her budding land. What a strange dream she had had. Warm runnels of recollection began to seep back to her. She turned her path toward her castle, small flowers, yellow clover and chamomile, springing up behind.

Across a meadow she saw a herdsman and his reindeer. She approached them thrilled with wonder and warmth, unable to understand why the herdsman fell trembling to his knees.

"Majesty, Majesty," the man said. "Please have mercy on me."

"Do you fear me?" she said in a voice so kind the man immediately looked up, astonished.

"All herdsmen fear Nova Zembla, Majesty. But our reindeer fatten finer here than on any pasture in the land."

"What is it that you fear, good man?"

"Forgive me. Forgive me. It is you, Your Majesty, and your eagles and the trolls."

"But I am of you," said the Princess. "I am not an eagle or a troll."

"You were, it is said, of us once, Majesty."

"Was and am again," said the Princess, feeling a sudden great liking for the herdsman and all his kind. "Though," she added, "I do not know how this came to be."

"Then we may graze here now in peace?" the herdsman said as he rose, hat in hand.

"You may," the Princess said, "and have no fear of me or the trolls. My eagles will see to the trolls. Trolls have no place in the world of men."

So began the slaughter of the trolls.

When the youngest troll slipped beneath his bridge with a reindeer calf across his back and found the Princess gone, he was fearful that another troll had carried her off. But he found no scent of other trolls about. Nor did he find a trace of the Princess' icy spoor: the smell of yellow clover and chamomile seared his nose. He looked both ways along the stream, then turned and loped off toward the castle, intending to search each cave and burrow until he found the Princess.

What he found were dead trolls, dozens of them, dropped from great heights by the twin sentry eagles. He heard the cry of a troll and saw him fall from the sky far upstream. The eagles were two specks in the sky. The youngest troll scrambled beneath a bush. Panting and hugging his knees, he tried to understand what he had done to anger the Princess so, but he could not. His troll instincts told him to run. So, starting that night, he began making his way toward the farthest reaches of Nova Zembla, to the place where the glaciers began.

As the end of thaw approached, herdsmen returning from the northmost pastures told of a single troll who lived at the edge of the ice, howled with the wolves at night but ran from men on sight.

"Then he must be the last," the Princess said. "And we will have him too, before the first snowfall."

She set out for the ice with her eagles, two reindeer, and a cart.

151

But the troll was not an easy prey. He slew the reindeer and carried them away and howled out on the ice at night. The last herdsmen begged the Princess to come away. Winter was hard by, they said. They had seen the Northern Lights.

The Princess refused. "I must make this place a place for men," she said. "I must be the one. No trolls will be left to harry men in Nova Zembla."

When the herdsmen had gone, the Princess took her birds and went out on the ice. In a raging bitter storm swirling down from the Pole, they found the troll burrowing into a drift of snow. Before he had the chance to cry out, the first eagle had swooped down and caught the troll in its crooked claws. The troll knew this was his end. He curled himself into the shape of warmth, the shape of a crude spoon.

That sight, that shape, brought a flood of memory to the Princess.

"No," she called, but the eagle was too high to hear, the wind too loud and rising. She called to the bird's mate to carry her aloft to call the other down. Tears froze on her face as she recalled the ugliness of the warm troll.

The birds carried the troll and the Princess higher and higher as the whirling storm spun them ever away from each other. In an instant, the troll knew what the Princess had done, and frozen in the shape of the only warmth he had ever known, he became the Big Dipper, pointing forever to the Princess we call the North Star.

Paul H. Williams
photo by Norman Snyder

Paul H. Williams was born in Tahlequah, Oklahoma. He attended schools in Arkansas, Oklahoma, and California, served in the Marine Corps in Vietnam, and received his B.A. and M.F.A. degrees from the University of Arkansas. He is the author of six action-adventure novels, one nonfiction account of a mass murderer, and a children's book based on Cherokee folk tales. His short fiction, poems, essays, articles, and reviews have appeared in a variety of periodicals, including *Arkansas Times, Arkansas Gazette, descant, The Grapevine, Greensboro Review, Preview,* and *Soldier of Fortune.* He has taught at the University of Arkansas, Flaming Rainbow University, and the Beijing Second Foreign Language Institute, and is the recipient of a Breadloaf Writer's Fellowship and an Arkansas Endowment for the Humanities Artist Grant. Mr. Williams is a citizen of the Cherokee Nation of Oklahoma and lives in Fayetteville, Arkansas, where he enjoys tennis, canoeing, and riding his antique motorcycle through the Ozark "twisties."